Murder on the Herald Express

To Heather and Tim Reed, with
best wishes,
            David

David Scott

Copyright © 2017 David Scott

ISBN: 978-1-326-97867-9

PublishNation
www.publishnation.co.uk

I am extremely grateful to my good friend Merrilyn Williams and my wife, Valerie, for taking the time and trouble to read the first draft and make a number of important suggestions with regard to writing style, structure and plot. This book would not have been the same without their input. However, any mistakes are mine alone.

Murder on the Herald Express is dedicated to many friends here in the United Kingdom and abroad, but particularly to life-long friend Stephen Robinson, best-selling author Duncan Hamilton, well travelled Pat Ducat, cricketing pal David Jones and football supporter David Morey.

A final dedication goes to Brian Foster who sadly died in 2016 and is sorely missed.

CHAPTER ONE

The unexpected mid morning telephone call was one that later he was to wish he had never received. It wasn't because it took him out of his comfort zone, which in itself was no bad thing, but the fact he had to face up to some unpalatable facts about his fellow journalists. The offer of a few weeks by the sea in a seaside resort where, or so he was told, manyana was the norm appeared on the surface to offer a welcome early summer break from the routine of keeping his current crop of newspaper editors on their toes.

For Dick Chinnery, editorial director for the Thompson Group of newspapers, a challenge every now and again made life interesting. It was just that nobody had told him murder was on the agenda.

He had impulsively agreed to 'help out' before he had had any time to think about it. "Ok, with me," had been his only reaction after his managing director and close friend Jack Wilde had asked if he would travel to Cornwall and take a look at a small group of newspapers the company had just purchased.

"They are a mixed bag of tabloids, mainly small weekly titles and one large bi-weekly, each making a small profit but badly in need of moving into the 1980s," Jack had informed him.

"Stay in a nice hotel, enjoy the food and do me a report as to both their potential and whether the existing staffs are up to the task, particularly the editors and journalists. I am sending you rather than anyone else in the company because I know you won't stand any nonsense. From what I have already heard and seen the people you will be dealing with are not the sharpest knives in the drawer."

It was a classic under-statement, as Dick was to discover.

It had been six years since that dreadful few weeks in 1979 when his world had been turned upside down. He had torn up just about every rule book while editing the Thurnham and Shaldon Standard but had managed, somehow, to expose Thurnham Council's masonic lodge and brought to an end a corrupt Town Hall regime before it could do any more damage.

His 'victory' though had come at a price. He had discovered his wife was having an affair with Toby Walters, a local estate agent who for a number of years had been the 'heavy' carrying out the necessary dirty work for the then council leader. When Toby and two of his friends went too far and badly beat up a rival councillor, they had also put one of Dick's reporters, Mary Lynch, in hospital. It had not taken the police long to bring charges and six months later Toby Walters had been provided with a new home courtesy of Her Majesty; somewhere he would stay for at least eight years. Or so Dick believed.

A few months later the council leader, chief executive and two other councillors were also given varying jail terms after corruption trials which effectively ended their careers in local government. After the judge delivered a withering indictment at the end of what - at the time - was a sensational trial several national newspapers and two local television stations had run their own exposes about the power wielded by other masonic lodges too closely associated with their local councils.

And it had all started in the small Essex town of Thurnham where until then the most dramatic stories had centred round fights at the annual flower show and who the mayor should invite to the civic dinner.

The tangled web of masonic friendships had even extended to Dick's own company chairman and managing director who had come close to having Dick sacked. It was only the 11th hour intervention of the company's owner, Henry Thompson, which had saved Dick not only from dismissal but a costly negligence legal action.

Dick had answered a summons to the company's headquarters in Torchester expecting to be met by the company's lawyers and be out of a job in quick time once the legal formalities were out of the way. Instead, he had been shocked into a rare silence when Henry and his the board of directors had told him Jack Wilde was the new managing director and would he like to become editorial director with responsibility for the management and editorial content of seven newspapers, not one? The previous chairman and managing director had been relieved of his position half an hour earlier.

When the board meeting had ended Jack had taken Dick on one side and revealed the part Dick's wife, Jenny, had played in recent events. She had been used by Toby Walters - perhaps even fallen in love with him - but what was not in doubt was she had been having an affair for several months at a time when Dick was working 14 hours a day to bring out the Standard during an eight week journalists' strike. The police had interviewed her under caution on several occasions, but ultimately they had concluded she had not committed any crime. The information she had passed on to Toby Walters and his fellow masons had made Dick's job more difficult, but there was no evidence to suggest she had been involved in, or knew about, the attack on the councillor and Mary. She had been a minor player in the overall scheme of things - a useful notch on Toby's bed post.

It had been all too much for Dick to take in at first, but he had controlled most of his emotions, at least in front of Jack. The conversation had moved on as to who should succeed him as the Standard's editor. He was not sure whether his very competent deputy would want to take over, but in the end they had agreed she should be offered the chance. Both men knew that if she took the job the switch could take place very quickly and allow Dick to head up the launch of a series of new free newspapers allied to their paid-for sister titles.

Change was in the air. If the Thompson Group did not launch their own free papers the monopoly they enjoyed in every town they served would be challenged by a new wave of newspaper entrepreneurs who did not always play by the established rules. Recent events that summer of 1979 had shown how vulnerable the company was to any attack.

Dick had known his marriage was in trouble before Jack Wilde had given him the full picture of what had been going on behind his back. He had felt partly to blame. He was single minded when it came to his work and the ill-advised national journalists' strike had triggered an overwhelming determination in him to bring out the Standard each week at the expense of everything else. When a rival free newspaper had been launched during the strike by a newspaper group from the East Midlands, which did not employ any journalists who were members of the journalists' union, it was like the proverbial red rag to his bull.

When he had analysed much later what had happened during those tumultuous months he had realised that his marriage had started to falter some time before. He and Jenny had drifted apart – were different people from the ones who had married seven years previously. She worked in an estate agent's office, had a different circle of friends and did not like socialising with anyone who had anything to do with newspapers. What really shocked him was that he had not had a single suspicion that she was having an affair. A combination of exposing what was going on at the Town Hall, the journalists' strike and the launch of a rival paper had relegated anything else in his mind to the back burner.

Dick had further complicated matters during those eight weeks. The Standard came out on time every Thursday thanks to the work done by the only reporter left in his office who due to an oversight had not been recruited into the journalists' union – Mary Lynch. The 38-year-old editor and 26-year-old reporter had worked side by side seven days a week to give the people of Thurnham and Shaldon their weekly diet of news and features.

She had been the first to realise she had fallen in love two weeks into the strike. It had scared her that she was willing to work such long hours simply because she enjoyed so much being near him and being part of her first great adventure in the newspaper world. He had been much slower to understand what was happening and it had only been during the last weekend of the strike, when they were both very tired and emotional, that things had developed.

As far as he knew nobody else was aware at that time their close working relationship during the journalists' strike had blossomed into something more, although the hospital manager at St Mary's must have suspected given the amount of time Dick spent at Mary's bedside while she was recovering from Toby Walters' vicious assault.

Anyway it didn't matter now. When Jack Wilde had told him his wife had been unfaithful for many months his own guilt vanished. Jenny had packed her bags and gone back to her family in Yorkshire. He didn't know what she had told them, but he didn't care. She didn't try to deny anything so their divorce went through quickly with the minimum of fuss. She had returned to Torchester to give evidence at Toby Walters' crown court trial, but she had stayed in a nearby hotel and as far as he knew had not ventured into Thurnham 20 miles away.

There was some sniggering round the town when the story of her infidelity featured in both the local and national newspapers' coverage of the trial, but it soon died down. The Daily Mail picture did not do her any favours.

Dick and Mary had married a year later by which time she was sat in his old editor's chair at the Thurnham and Shaldon Standard and he was her boss – at least at work. The deputy had not enjoyed being a number one and had been happy to revert to her old role.

It had been five interesting years since. All the Thompson newspapers had built up a reputation for good, solid, accurate, reliable journalism backed up by advertising departments trained to deliver quality customer service. Economically Essex and Suffolk had not suffered as much as other parts of the country from Margaret Thatcher's 1979 General Election victory and by 1985 not only had the newspapers serving the coastal strip and wealthy towns seen annual growth and healthy profit margins, they had been perfectly placed to take advantage of the wage explosion and housing boom when the south east was first to come out of a national recession. Some weeks the larger weekly papers in the group struggled to find room for all the job adverts.

The only surprise, as far as Dick was concerned, was the fact Henry Thompson, now in his late eighties, had bought another independent newspaper group 350 miles away. When Jack Wilde gave him two folders containing all the information he would need it was obvious that somewhere along the line Henry was doing an old pal a favour by buying his newspapers. So it was to turn out.

When he was alone Dick sat down and started to read what Jack had given him. He immediately burst out laughing. Jack had clipped a note to the front of the file and on it was written: '*Make sure you get to the bottom of this!*' Bottom was underlined. Dick had never holidayed in Cornwall. He knew where Plymouth and Exeter were, having visited them while holidaying on the south Devon coast, but where was Broad Bottom?

This had to be some sort of joke Jack was having at his expense, he thought.

'*The Broad Bottom Herald Express group of newspapers covers all the Bottoms*' said the briefing note.

A quick look at his book of maps confirmed there was indeed a Broad Bottom on the Cornish coast and nearby were the villages of Great Bottom, Snail's Bottom, Rainbow Bottom, Little Bottom and Six Wells Bottom. He really had been given a bum job!

When he got home that night and told Mary she could not stop giggling. She was still shaking when she passed him a beer and said: 'Bottoms up!'

It did not take Dick long on Monday morning to rearrange his diary for the coming few weeks and deal with his administration. He went through what needed to be done with his secretary, Margaret Evans, who had followed him to Torchester when he stepped down as editor of the Thurnham and Shaldon Standard to become editorial supremo at head office. She bossed him even more than his wife and probably knew what he wanted, what he would say and how he would do things more than anyone else in the company. He knew she would open his daily post, keep him informed of anything important and generally 'look after the shop'. He trusted her implicitly. He knew none of his editors would dare step out of line in his absence while Margaret was keeping an eye on them – never mind Jack.

He decided to risk using the M25, even though it had yet to be completed in two short sections, and soon found himself on the A12 heading west. When he joined the motorway at Brentwood he had a relatively easy non-stop but slow drive through the Dartford tunnel beneath the River Thames. Traffic was not particularly heavy and in under two hours he was on the M3 which led him onto the A303 near Andover. A stop for coffee and two poached eggs at a Little Chef gave him a timely boost and a chance to stretch his legs. Apart from the expected crawl past Stonehenge he was able to eat up the miles in his four litre Rover as it sped over Salisbury Plain and on into the westcountry. The views on a bright, sunny day were stunning. He had no way of knowing but the storm clouds were gathering elsewhere.

CHAPTER TWO

When word reached the journalists working on the bi-weekly Broad Bottom Herald Express that they should expect a visit soon from the editorial director of the company which had just bought out their ageing previous owner, Harvey Fairbanks, it was decided a lunch-time meeting was called for. Nobody was a member of any union – not even those working on the press or production side. Three weeks before they had hardly looked up from their typewriters when they were told there would be a flying visit that day from a couple of men in smart suits who had duly looked round the different offices and then disappeared into the boardroom. Everyone assumed some sort of valuation was being done into the worth of their office. A few hoped they would soon move into better accommodation; nobody guessed the real reason behind the inspection.

Ten days later they found out when much to their astonishment they were told the company had been sold and a deal had been struck to incorporate them into the Thompson Newspaper Group based in Essex. They were given no promises apart from a bald statement saying all existing terms and conditions would remain in force and further information would be supplied as soon as possible.

They knew nothing about their new owners, apart from the fact they were not part of one of the big regional newspaper operations like Northcliffe, Westminster Press or Reed International. Tucked away in a quiet backwater of the country, they didn't know much about any other newspaper group because they had no real competition except that provided by the daily Western Morning News, based far away in Plymouth, who showed only the occasional interest in Broad Bottom.

"The old man pulled a fast one there," muttered chief reporter Tony Morrisey when they had gathered in what passed for a rest room but was also their kitchen.

"I don't blame him for selling up at his age, but you would have thought he would have told us and given us a slice of the cake."

Several of the older members of staff nodded their heads in agreement, but not Edna Sparrow, the editorial secretary, who was far too street wise to believe Harvey Fairbanks or his now ex-managing director son, Herbert, would give anybody a penny more than they had to. She kept her peace for the time being. She knew Tony was full of wind and if shove ever came to push he could not be relied on to take any decisive action.

He tipped his cap to anyone senior, but tried, mainly unsuccessfully, in various ways to bully anyone junior. As their line boss he did a competent enough job at a pace which totally suited the rest of the team – slow.

It wasn't until Tim Fletcher, the group's senior editor, came and joined them ten minutes later that anything meaningful was imparted.

"I have made some phone calls and discovered our visitor will be a certain Dick Chinnery who some of you who weren't still at school six years ago might recall made a name for himself nationally when he produced a large weekly paper for eight weeks with the help of his now wife during the last journalists' strike."

There was silence round the room.

"What we have to do is convince Mr Chinnery we are competent enough to be left alone to our own devices and that 700 mile round trips to see what we are up to are only worth undertaking a couple of times a year – if that. Whatever you might think about old Harvey I am sure he has told our new masters what a great team we are, what superb papers we produce and how we always go the extra yard. Well, he will have done if he had any sense and wanted a big cheque in return."

There were a few laughs. He had their attention now.

"I understand Mr Chinnery won't just be looking at our editorial operation, but will be taking a close look at the advertising, production staffs and press crew. Let's make sure he finds more than enough to keep him occupied elsewhere."

They all agreed, but had no idea how they would do it. Anyway, some of them concluded, with a combination of ignorance and arrogance, what does someone from Essex know about producing newspapers in Cornwall?

They would soon find out.

While the reporters made a variety of hot drinks and saw an opportunity to chat rather than work, Tim left to speak to his fellow editors, both of whom managed two weekly titles each of which had small but reasonable paginations. The Herald Express was the group's flagship and main revenue earner, but between them the Crackington by Sea Gazette, Piddle Wood Times, Tinkerbush News and Upperthong Observer made small but important financial contributions to overall group profits. They were long established community newspapers with no serious competition.

When the rest of the news room eventually went back to writing up their golden wedding, obituaries and parish council meeting reports it was Edna Sparrow who spent longer than anybody else worrying about the future. She never revealed her true feelings to anyone in the news room, but she could sense change was in the air and the comfort zone they had enjoyed for as long as she could remember was about to be threatened. It simply would not do!

Tim had his own worries. He had come up through the ranks and after working hard to become the Herald's editor had created what he thought was the perfect job to suit his easy going lifestyle. In his youth he had been a very good tennis player with huge potential. He represented Cornwall at every age level, but never made it into the professional ranks. However, the Broad Bottom Tennis Club was his private empire and for the last two years he had run a thriving tennis school at the club which paid him handsomely. Every week he divided his time between the newspaper and the tennis school, leaving many decisions on the former to his hard working deputy, Claire, Tony and the rest.

He had been careful to make sure he never missed the really important meetings with Harvey and the advertising manager and so far nobody had challenged him about the increasing amount of time he was spending away from the office. Naively, some of the reporters thought he was an old fashioned editor who liked to spend part of each day in the pub. After all, wasn't that what they had always been taught about where to find the best stories? How clever of him not to come back to the office late in the afternoon smelling of beer!

He did nothing to disabuse them, but he knew Harvey Fairbanks' out-of-the-blue decision to sell the Herald Express and his other newspapers had the potential to challenge his comfortable status quo. He didn't like the thought of what it would mean if he was to come under the scrutiny of an experienced editorial director, especially one who had already shown he was no pushover and was not afraid to work long hours. It simply would not do!

Nobody took much notice of Rufus Jones if they could help it. He only worked three days a week out of choice, spending the other two days writing feature articles for magazines nobody had ever heard of. He had tried to freelance full time but there was not enough work in Cornwall to pay the bills and leave a goodly amount over for beer money. Rufus made most people feel uncomfortable. They could not tell you why, but he was somebody who looked and acted shifty even when he was making a cup of tea. Rufus was permanently unhappy - even more so today. He had a nasty feeling his life had just taken a turn for the worse. It simply would not do!

*

They did not know when to expect Dick. He ensured before he left Torchester that neither Jack Wilde nor anyone else informed any of the Herald Express's managers of his impending arrival. The long journey down the A303 gave him ample time to evaluate what he had read in Jack's file. Profit margins on all six papers were low compared with what the Thompson Group was making in the south east, but he was experienced enough to know that there was less advertising to be had in the westcountry in several key areas including the lucrative jobs market. He was not surprised the estate agents took between 20 and 36 pages in the Friday edition of the Herald Express and between 12 and 16 pages in the smaller weeklies, but if they were anything like the crooks he had dealt with in Thurnham six years ago it was odds on they weren't paying much for their advertising. He chided himself when he remembered that it was several respectable 'rebel' estate agents along with Henry Thompson who had saved his job and reputation.

'I must keep an open mind' he said out loud just as he turned off the A38 and headed to the coast.

The Royal Imperial Hotel overlooking a long beach was a welcome sight after his seven hour drive. He was given a large double bedroom with an equally large bathroom which contained a mix of elegant soaps, expensive shampoos and a dressing gown. He didn't delay ringing his wife who he knew would still be at work getting ready that week's Standard – her deadline was 24 hours away.

"I miss you already" were the words he wanted to hear and Mary didn't disappoint him. He told her all about the wonderful views every time he came over the top of a hill on the A303 and promised she could come with him one week if he discovered he needed to spend more time in Broad Bottom than he really wanted to.

A second call to his secretary was shorter and to the point. All was well. She had refused, on his behalf, a couple of dinner invitations and three requests to speak to different organisations in the next month. The other editors had not been told yet where he had gone – as far as they were concerned he was either at a four day conference or playing golf with a bunch of advertisers in Scotland.

He was up before seven the next morning and after showering had time to enjoy a brisk 15 minute walk along the sea wall before shocking the Royal Imperial's breakfast team who were used to their more elderly clientele drifting down from 8.30 onwards. He ate a hearty breakfast which was personally cooked for him. He was glad there were no grease filled and fat soaked metal turines containing fried eggs, burnt sausages and dried up bacon.

It was just before 8.30 when he turned into the Herald Express car park situated at the far end of an industrial estate which looked at first glance as though it contained a number of old aircraft hangers converted into offices. He hoped the insides were more cheerful than their exteriors.

The car park contained one other car belonging to the man he later discovered was responsible for ensuring newsagents in the main towns were well stocked with papers and the free delivery teams really did their jobs. He was loading bundles of the Tuesday edition of the Herald Express into the back of his Volvo estate. After Dick satisfied him that he really was a representative of the new owners, he stepped into the reception area, looked around to get his bearings and then moved quickly on through the side door to the editorial department. It looked a mess with cluttered desks and old newspapers littering the floor. The smell was not something he had experienced before – a mixture of stale food, sweat and body odour. He wondered whether Jack Wilde already knew what a state the office was in, but had decided that rather than warn him he would let Dick draw his own conclusions.

He needed to see what the other departments were like. The advertising department was nowhere near as bad, probably because it was mainly staffed by women, or so he surmised. The production department was laid out as he expected with rows of large boards containing pages half ready while awaiting final completion later that day before their journey to the press room below. It was orderly and looked as though it was well managed. Further exploration brought him to the toilets, then the 'dark room' where the photographers did their internal work and a couple of store rooms. His keen sense of smell took him to the kitchen/rest room where he found a sink full of cups all of which were coated with inner brown rings. The fridge contained many items which were well out of date, while after taking one look at the milk he decided to have his tea black – if he was offered a cup.

The office was still empty so he opened the boardroom door and made himself at home. This, he quickly decided, was going to be his base over the next few weeks. There were three internal windows which allowed him to see out into the editorial department in one direction, the advertising department in the other and directly out to the reception area through the smaller third window. It was perfect. He doubted whether anyone would notice him until he made his presence known.

It was two minutes before nine when the rush started. Nobody seemed to be in a hurry to do any work, but for a few moments the reception area was full. Over the next 10 minutes there was a regular flow of newcomers. He gave it a few more minutes before stepping out of the boardroom when the first thing he noticed was the overwhelming smell of bacon. He had intended to seek out Tim Fletcher first, but a combination of the smell and the noise coming from the kitchen were irresistible. So engrossed were more than a dozen people in either chatting, cooking or making tea and coffee that at first nobody noticed him.

Two women brushed past him without saying a word, but eventually he was challenged by a man eating a sausage sandwich with a none-too-friendly: "Can I help you?"

Dick decided to play for time.

"I am just doing an office check on behalf of the new owners," which seemed to satisfy the man who was more concerned about his failure to stop tomato sauce dripping onto his shirt.

Dick retreated back to the boardroom from where he could watch what happened next. By his calculation two people were working in the advertising department, five or six scruffy looking reporters were sat in front of their typewriters and two girls on reception were helping sort out the post overlooked by a middle-aged smartly dressed woman whom he guessed just had to be the editorial secretary. She snatched one of the piles and marched off back to a desk which had the only orderly look about it. He was right.

Two men stood chatting – he guessed by their appearance and the way they were grumbling they were photographers. A few others wandered round the two rooms at varying times over the next half hour. Dick watched and waited.

Just before ten o'clock the kitchen emptied and what seemed like a small army descended on their desks in the advertising department and begin to make telephone calls. He marvelled at how regimented it all was.

It was time to make himself known, starting with reception. There was no point in getting angry with the two girls when he told them who he was and asked to see the signing-in book. He was not surprised to discover that his was the first name to be entered that morning. A quick glance told him either the Herald Express had very few visitors or the signing-in book was rarely used.

"How would you know who was in the building if there was a fire?" he asked.

He was met with stony silence.

It was something he was to get used to in the coming weeks.

They did not try to stop him as he took the door to the editorial department, but they exchanged worried looks. The awful smell he had noticed earlier assailed his nostrils, made worse by the extra cooking smells from that morning's breakfast.

"I have come to see Tim Fletcher," he told the first reporter to lift his head up and catch his eye.

"He isn't in yet," came the rasping reply.

Before Dick could respond the door opened behind him and the editor walked in.

CHAPTER THREE

It had not been a good morning for Tim Fletcher. He had slept badly, two people had cancelled tennis lessons for later in the day because they had 'child-minding problems' and he had dealt with a number of minor problems at the tennis club involving plumbing and maintenance. To top it all the drive to the office had taken longer than usual because of roadworks. He was not in a positive frame of mind and totally unprepared for Dick Chinnery. As he headed for his office at the far end of the room he realised he was being asked a question.

"Mr Fletcher, I presume?"

An internal warning bell rang immediately. He turned to look at the man in the dark suit he had passed without giving him a second glance and realised in a split second this had to be his new editorial director. He knew his morning had just taken a huge turn for the worse.

"Yes, and you must be Mr Chinnery. Nobody told me to expect you this morning,"

"Obviously not," was Dick's sardonic reply.

He gave Tim one of those dangerous looks which everybody in Torchester knew meant they would be well advised to watch out and choose their words carefully.

The Herald's editor was saved, for the time being at least, by his secretary. Edna Sparrow jumped up to ask if Dick wanted a cup of tea or coffee. *At least somebody in this office is alert*, he thought.

Edna looked him straight in the eye while he weighed up his options. She, for one, was not going to be bullied or thrown out of her stride.

"Thank you, a black coffee with one sugar in a clean cup would be nice - if you can fight your way through the crowd in the kitchen."

The point was not lost on Tim who ushered Dick into his office where a pile of opened post, several reporters' expenses sheets and a couple of boxes of tennis balls sat on his desk.

"The electrical garage door was playing up this morning."

Tim knew it sounded lame, offering an excuse before he had even been challenged about his time-keeping. He had done it before when faced with a difficult situation. He inwardly groaned. Would he never learn that there were times when saying very little was a virtue?

"Happen often?" retorted Dick just as Edna came in with his coffee. To his disappointment there was no biscuit in his saucer. He made a mental note to buy some ginger nuts.

Tim wasn't given the chance to offer up another feeble reply.

Dick thanked Edna but took note that her cold stare seemed to be a permanent fixture.

Without seeking Tim's permission he told her: "I am going to be using the boardroom while I am here so can you check the diary and re-arrange any meetings anyone has planned from Monday morning through to Thursday afternoon until I indicate otherwise? I won't be here on Fridays."

She signalled she understood.

"I want to speak to everyone in the editorial and advertising departments at eleven o'clock today. And I really do mean eleven o'clock," added Dick.

The point was no lost on either Tim or Edna. His other editors in East Anglia would have smiled. They knew from bitter experience that the one thing they never did when Dick Chinnery called a meeting was turn up late without a very good reason.

"Please arrange for the journalists to walk through and sit with their advertising colleagues. The production and press managers should also attend, but I don't want to disrupt their departments too much. I will also need a full staff list with job titles."

Edna nodded and left. She wasn't a woman who wasted many words, but when she got back to her desk she now felt she knew what sort of man she was going to be dealing with in the coming days. She also knew she had even more cause to be worried.

"Is there anything you would like to ask me before the meeting?" Dick asked Tim.

He waited for all of three seconds.

"If not, I will let you get started on your working day. I will try not to interfere with production of the papers, but there will be times when I will need you to answer my questions as they arise."

And with that he was out of the editor's office and halfway across the news room before there was any opportunity for Tim to respond.

Tim stared at the opposite wall. It was worse than he had ever expected. Then he realised that when Harvey Fairbanks had told him he had sold up he had never given much thought to what the future might hold for him personally. It was time that he did.

*

It was not difficult to spot which department people came from, thought Dick, when he addressed them. At least the advertising reps dressed presentably. He had no intention of giving too much away about future plans at this stage and limited himself to some background on the Thompson Newspaper Group and the standards it expected from all its staff. He informed them that in due course a new managing director would arrive, but in the short term they were to regard him as their senior manager.

"If there are any outstanding issues I should know about I want to hear about them in the next three days. If I don't, and it later comes out that you knew, it will be a serious disciplinary offence. I hope you take the hint that I expect honesty and openness. In return you will find your new company is a good employer and you will have a bright future."

He fielded a couple of innocuous questions, none of them from a journalist. They were either keeping their powder dry or thought he would disappear in an easterly direction quicker than he had come. It prompted him to make one thing very clear.

"I have a terrible reputation when dealing with people who turn up late. If I say I want to see somebody at 10am, I really do mean 10am."

And with that he let them drift back to their desks. Tim blanched.

Now was the time for Dick to talk to the advertisement manager after which he would set about improving the reporters' sartorial image. He wasn't to know that would prove in the long run to be the least of his concerns.

CHAPTER FOUR

While Dick was getting to know some of the people at the Broad Bottom Herald Express, 250 miles away in the House of Commons selected guests were being entertained to lunch in the Members' Dining Room, by far the best and most exclusive room available if you could afford it.

As Marie-Clementine Dubois was aware it was not only the largest and versatile event venue in the House of Commons, but also the most sought after. If somebody wanted to impress, and on this day in particular she and her boyfriend Ryan Johnston were definitely out to do just that, they could not have selected anywhere better.

Their guests included nine members of Parliament from both main parties, four lords, three senior policemen, half a dozen senior civil servants, five Fleet Street editors, a variety of diplomats and a good selection of very attractive women. They were escorted to a room adorned with beautiful flock wallpaper, wooden relief sculptures and fascinating paintings. The ornate Royal Coat of Arms sat proudly above the main entrance signifying the connection of the Monarchy to Parliament.

Once intended as a conference room known as the 'Painted Chamber' the Members' Dining Room provided the perfect space for the mingling and gossip which flowed over the first couple of rounds of drinks. Marie-Clementine stood at the door taking in the scene, aware that she had chosen well.

Ryan Johnston knew all of the policemen. He was their superior in rank, if not within their individual forces, as the number two to East Anglia's Chief Constable. He was on first name terms with most of their English guests, but only time would tell how well he would get to know some of the diplomats. And that was why he and Marie-Clementine were being paid a lot of money by the people they represented to set up The Tuesday Club right under Margaret Thatcher's nose.

Marie-Clementine attracted men and she knew it. It didn't take long before Mohamed Osman from the Egyptian Embassy engaged her in the first of what she knew would be a series of boring but possibly useful conversations. She had the gift of appearing to listen to every word while staring into someone's eyes without attempting to understand what was being said, unless it concerned matters of defence. Even then anyone she was engaged in conversation with would not have spotted the occasional twinkle in her eye when she heard something indiscreet elsewhere. She cast her eyes round the room and was satisfied all was well.

She thought Jurgen Weber from the East German Embassy was much more interesting and far more attractive than the Egyptian from whom she eventually managed to disengage herself. She knew he was a high ranking member of the Stasi, the official state security service of the German Democratic Republic and one of the most effective and professional intelligence services in the world. Of course, for official purposes, he was a member of a trade mission. Marie-Clementine knew better.

He was too well mannered and experienced to talk about anything but trade when he was with her and one of the civil servants who joined them, but she was glad that at the lunch table she had placed him next to one of the Conservative MPs who just happened to be chairman of the House of Commons Defence Committee.

The newspaper editors were a useful hard-drinking bunch who could be guaranteed to liven up any lunch-time or even late afternoon session. The more they drank the more absurd they became. They were present on strict lobby terms so anything they gleaned was non-attributable.

For Ryan and Marie-Clementine they were cover. It had been a clever suggestion from one of their paymasters to compromise them – just in case it was ever needed. Other London editors would be invited to future lunches where they would be welcome to 'take home' one of the girls or mix their alcohol intake with something which gave them a real short-term boost.

For those who knew them Ryan Johnston and Marie-Clementine Dubois were an unusual couple. Everybody could understand what he saw in her, but few could work out what she, aged 30 and 22 years younger, saw in him. They had met two years ago when she had spent six months working as an assistant secretary to an elderly Tory MP. Tall, attractive with short red hair, she turned heads within any room she entered. Her father was a French diplomat who had died in a skiing accident when she was 14. Her mother had died of cancer two years later. As an only child she had inherited enough money to keep her in a style she had now grown accustomed to. An expensive private school in Switzerland had completed her education and introduced her to several useful contacts.

34

Ryan had fallen in love with Marie-Clementine within minutes of meeting her at a House of Commons reception for senior police officers, despite the fact he was married with two grown-up daughters.

His wife, Annabel, had not been too disappointed when she had found out that her marriage was to all intents and purposes over. She had been more surprised when he had left the family home in Chelmsford three months later and had let her know that if all went well with their pending divorce he hoped to re-marry fairly soon after.

She had made some enquiries of her own and had been surprised and a little shocked he had been seen with a vivacious but much younger French woman. Somehow his slippers and cardigan image did not sit right with that, but when she confided in a female friend over a glass of wine she realised it was just another example of how opposites can attract.

Marie-Clementine bit into a vol-au-vent, finished it off and decided the time had come for her to signal everyone should sit down and enjoy the main courses. The food was good, but that was of secondary importance to her. The wine was even more expensive; it flowed copiously. She spotted that two Members of Parliament had already taken something that was stronger than an aspirin.

Sergei Mudkoi, the only Russian present, was charm personified. He drank very little and while everyone tucked into what they all agreed was a superb beef wellington, he made regular eye contact with Jurgen. They worked as a team and would share a brandy later in the day to compare notes.

James Fitz-Lloyd Smythe, an ex environment minister and now a junior minister of defence, had a view on just about every subject on the sun and was not afraid to voice it throughout the lunch – no matter whose company he shared.

"Margaret and your president will sort out the Ruskies, mark my words," he told Don Bryant, an American businessman.

"I have seen the minutes of their recent meetings. You gave us far more help in the Falklands than it is diplomatic to make too public."

Excellent, thought Marie-Clementine. *Just the sort of cosy discussion to make life interesting for some of my guests.*

She hoped there would be many more.

One senior policeman, however, was far from pleased with what he was hearing. Arthur Nightingale, newly appointed deputy commissioner of the Met and unknown in London social circles, was careful not to let anyone see he was hardly touching the alcohol offered him. His gin and tonic was much, much more of the latter. Everybody thought he was Jason Pearce, chairman of British Aerospace, who had travelled down from Preston especially to attend the lunch. The real Jason Pearce had not found it difficult to forego the pleasure and let Arthur take his place.

Arthur's boss, the fraud squad and MI5 were very interested in Miss Dubois. As for Deputy Chief Constable Johnston, his card had already been well and truly marked after he chose to ignore a friendly warning from the very top about the people he was mixing with socially. If he married Miss Dubois he would not be given any other option but to resign when he was shown the file the security services were building on her.

In the meantime Arthur, out of uniform, was happy to try and find out what The Tuesday Club would get up to next and who was really financing it. He floated in and out of various conversations without saying anything much. His excellent hearing, however, left him under no illusions about some of the topics being discussed.

CHAPTER FIVE

Although he had come up through the ranks via the editorial route, Dick Chinnery was well versed in the commercial side of the newspaper business. Between them Henry Thompson and Jack Wilde had ensured over the preceding six years that not only did he now know about advertising yields per page, or even per centimetre, rate cards, discounts and how to hit targets in the all-important situations vacant section, but the diverse workings of the production staff and press crew plus their union bosses had been drummed into him both on the job and at private meetings. He had enjoyed the learning curve, capped off by a month of management training at the world famous Ashridge College.

After the staff meeting the delightfully named Lulu Popplewell followed him into the boardroom. She was the Herald's senior advertising manager.

"You didn't tell us much," she said.

He smiled. His file had already told him Lulu would not be a problem. His job was to reassure her, while making sure she understood that reporting procedures needed to change.

"I am going to get straight to the point, Lulu. For the time being Henry Thompson is happy with the advertising targets he saw prior to buying the company. What he and I are not sure about is whether you and your team were consulted and whether they are realistic. I have a copy for you. I want an honest answer when you have studied the figures."

He handed over a blue file. Lulu gingerly took it.

"You ought to know that half a million pounds has been held in reserve from the sale price just in case these figures are incorrect, or if there are too many uncollectable bad debts. Harvey Fairbanks will not get his final cheque for at least six months."

Lulu nodded. Wisely, he reflected, she did not comment. Instinctively he felt he could trust her.

"There is one further thing I want you to tackle with immediate effect. I shall be telling Tim Fletcher as well, but I think it is your staff who will be most affected. If we pay people to start work at nine o'clock I expect just that. I am not against anyone coming in and having their breakfast in the kitchen, but not in company time. If there is a problem with the extractor fans get someone to fix them because I don't want the office smelling like a transport cafe all day long. If anyone thinks this is unfair ask them to see me."

He wasn't out to win any popularity contest – simply determined to put down a marker on day one.

"There is another option they can consider if they wish – they can be paid for five hours less work!"

When Lulu left he started to explore the boardroom's cupboards and found what he wanted – a couple of clean mugs plus a tray of decent cups and saucers, a plug in kettle and several packets of plain biscuits. From another cupboard he selected copies of the last four editions of each paper and settled down with a notepad to read them.

They weren't bad, if a tad boring. There was plenty of what he called bread and butter material – weddings, obituaries, golden weddings, fetes and fayres, plus numerous council and court stories. His eagle eye spotted too many stories which looked as though they had been retyped from press releases without any attempt to develop them, and a couple of times he winced when he spotted poor punctuation or grammar. Nor was he surprised when he discovered certain councillors got their names into each edition on too many occasions and a picture of Broad Bottom's Mayor visiting some event or other popped up on a regular basis every week. He knew he would have to do a lot more reading before he could come to any conclusions, but if his initial impressions were correct the

Herald Express in particular was in its own little comfort zone, and barely kicked up much fuss about anything. He had yet to meet the other two editors, but he hoped they would not turn out to be 'steady Eddies'. He was looking for drive and flair.

One story in the Herald Express a month ago did catch his eye though. The first deaconess appointed by any Anglican church in Cornwall had been sacked only eight months into her role. The story claimed the deaconess was 'visiting family in another part of the country' and the church was refusing to comment, but several parishioners had been prepared to go on the record to say they were demanding answers from their bishop and were very unhappy. The following week the Herald had managed to track down the deaconess and there was a follow up story from an interview given by her and the new love in her life – the wife of a policeman in Essex. He made a mental note to check later in the day if the Herald Express had carried any more stories about the two women in future editions.

It's a story we should follow up back home, thought Dick.

He put in a call to the editor of the Torchester Evening Gazette and after telling him the main points of the Herald's stories asked to be kept informed of any developments before carefully separating the relevant pages from the rest of the two papers and tucking them into his briefcase.

It was a good job he was looking out of the right hand window just at that moment otherwise he would not have spotted the sandwich van parked outside the front door. *Welcome to Cornwall*, he thought.

He was not bothered he had not been offered another cup of tea or coffee all morning – he was used to making his own and at least this way he knew what would be in the cups – but the failure of anyone to tell him about the sandwich van when as far as he knew there wasn't a cafe or shop within two miles was a clear indication that nobody in this office at least was going to make life easy or comfortable for him. "Sobeit," he muttered under his breath. For the next hour he continued reading and taking notes until he was interrupted by a phone call.

"Enjoying yourself in sunny Cornwall," was Jack Wilde's greeting.

"It is good to hear a friendly voice," he replied. "Just how much would you like me to sort out in the first 72 hours?"

"Why do you think I sent you and not somebody else? We had to get a return at some stage on all that expensive management training we have given you."

Dick updated him on all that had happened that morning. For a few moments there was silence at the other end of the line.

"Ok, I get the picture loud and clear even from 350 miles away. I will brief Henry this afternoon, but I see no reason why you shouldn't start to sort things out right away. You don't have to cover your back here, but I think you should ring me every evening from your hotel so I can keep abreast of things."

Dick never interrupted his boss when he was in full flow.

"Let's just say that I am not surprised and suspect we don't know one half of what is going on at the Broad Bottom Herald Express. If we have to get rid of the lot of them we will do it in the coming months, starting with those at the top," added Jack.

He changed tack. "The main reason I rang was to tell you I need you to take the monthly editors' meeting here in Torchester on Friday because I will be attending a funeral. But I will be back in time for us to have a longer chat in mid afternoon."

Dick laughed. "And there's me thinking you were worried about my health," he said.

He heard Jack chuckle. "I suggest you give them hell in the south west the rest of today and tomorrow, pop in to the Broad Bottom office first thing on Thursday to ensure they all turn up on time and then have a leisurely drive back to Essex. The traffic should not be too bad on a Thursday. By the way, I think in future weeks you should fly from Stansted to RAF St Mawgan near Newquay and take a taxi to the office. They have enough pool cars for you to grab one when needed. That should ease your stress levels and keep you sharp for the tasks ahead."

Dick knew that he was being cared for as much as he could be by his long-time friend and boss. He didn't fancy regular seven hour drives from Essex to Cornwall and back on his own every week. It would be even longer if there were any hold-ups.

Ten minutes after talking with Jack he phoned Margaret Evans and discovered she had already found out the times of flights on Mondays and Thursdays for him - they were perfect. She asked him a few questions about different items in his post which enabled him to brief her on the necessary replies and leave the rest in her more than capable hands. The last thing he needed was too much work stacking up back at base.

He was just about to leave the boardroom and make his first trip through to the production department and on to the press room when Tim Fletcher came in without knocking. He carried several copies of his own paper.

"You asked me to let you know if there were any outstanding issues."

Dick looked at him but did not comment.

"In the post this morning I received a letter from a firm of London solicitors threatening to sue the Herald Express for defamation concerning a couple of recent stories."

Somehow Dick knew this was not going to be good news. It was something he could well do without.

"You better shut the door and show me which stories so I can decide how we should react," he told the Herald's editor.

Tim laid his papers on the boardroom table and immediately turned to the stories about the deaconess.

"Surely the church aren't threatening us with a libel action?" asked Dick.

"No, but they have made their displeasure known to my chief reporter. It's the husband of the woman our deaconess has fallen in love with. He is claiming we have defamed him on two consecutive weeks. To make matters worse he appears to be somebody very high up in the East Anglian Constabulary. He has engaged very expensive solicitors who probably charge a fortune by the hour."

Dick sat down and read far more carefully the stories Tim had brought with him. He didn't like some of the reporting or the loose phraseology. When he compared what had been written with what the solicitor's letter contained, he could immediately see where the newspaper might have an expensive problem.

He had met Deputy Chief Constable Ryan Johnston on a couple of occasions, but exchanged no more than passing pleasantries.

"You quote Mrs Johnston in this story as saying her marriage is all but over because her policeman husband has had a string of affairs including one with a French woman who is making a name for herself in London social circles."

Once again Tim reacted without thinking: "Yes, but we didn't name them so there shouldn't be a problem."

It took all of Dick's self control to stay calm. Those who knew him well learned to recognise the times when he was most angry; on such occasions the look in his eyes was either one of cold fury or contempt. On this occasion it was the latter.

"You don't have to name somebody to defame them if they can prove that the words you have used could be reasonably understood to refer to them. Indeed, you could face multiple legal actions because several people could claim the words referred to them"

Tim blanched.

"I want to see all your reporter's notes and God help us if his shorthand is not very good. I don't care how late you have to work tonight because I want them transcribed, typed up and ready for me to read first thing in the morning.

"I suggest you ring our legal people in Essex immediately, brief them and leave nothing out. I want cuttings faxed to them this afternoon along with the threatening letter. I will see what they have to say before asking them to respond on your behalf. Have I got all the stories here or are there more?"

Tim produced a two page spread from last Friday's Herald Express.

"I think we might also have a problem with this."

Dick could not believe it. The deaconess and policeman's wife had been the male and female lead in last December's church pantomime. A freelance photographer, who had been asked to attend one of the rehearsals, had retained the copyright and in return for a promise of future regular weekend work had handed them over to the Herald Express. The pictures included plenty of children.

"I am just about to return a call from the Press Council," spluttered Tim. "I think they have received a complaint with regard to invasion of privacy and the use of the children's photos."

Dick was not in a mood to offer any comfort. "It's not your day, is it?" was his retort. "Ring the solicitors first, then the Press Council. I will be here until six o'clock; update me before you leave.

Damn it, thought Tim, *I have four tennis lessons arranged, the first one starting at five o'clock.* He phoned his wife and asked her to cancel all of them.

"Say I have a bad cold and do not want to pass it on," he snapped.

Two cups of tea later and after much thought about what Tim Fletcher had shown him Dick felt it was about time he wandered into the production area and then find the press room. He passed through both the advertising and editorial departments without anyone impeding his progress. He could sense their resentment over his breakfast edict. At least the pre-press room looked busy with skilled machinists typing up stories and preparing the adverts to be pasted onto the multitude of pages laid out on boards stretching as far as the eye could see.

"You must be Mr Chinnery," chimed the first cheerful voice he had heard with a Cornish accent. "I am Frank Helliwell, production manager and in charge of this motley crew. Welcome to Broad Bottom."

Dick did not want to linger very long and after a few pleasantries asked Frank to set aside an hour next Monday so they could get to know each other better.

He was just about to walk through to the press room when Frank grabbed his arm and said: "They are cleaning the press and doing maintenance. They don't like to be disturbed."

Dick freed his arm and gave the production manner a look which said '*don't dare do that again*'.

"I am only going to introduce myself to them because I know they will be busy the rest of the week printing the different papers."

Frank thought about putting out his arm again and then changed his mind.

"Only three of them are in at the moment."

Dick was mystified.

"How many should there be?"

"A full crew is six, but there is quite a bit of sickness about."

Dick was not fooled. Here was another little mystery he would get to the bottom of. However, at the moment he had more than enough to occupy his mind for one day. There was a time and a place for everything.

When he returned to the boardroom he did not see Edna Sparrow leave her desk and go through to the production department. After Frank told her what had transpired she was even more worried. This really was not going well.

Tim Fletcher reported back to Dick just before five o'clock to say everything he had requested had gone to the company's retained legal expert Richard Orange at Root's, the Torchester law firm.

"They have agreed to send what will be a holding letter to the policeman's legal representative tomorrow. In the meantime I have been urged to ensure everything which might be used in our defence is put under lock and key. He suggests you and I have a friendly meeting with the policeman's wife and her new partner to see if they can be of help," said the editor.

At that moment there was an audible din in reception as the clock struck five. Dick had rarely seen so many people move so fast. They were out of the door, across the car park and away in a cloud of exhaust fumes before he realised the office was nearly deserted.

"I presume you won't be leaving just yet?" he enquired.

Tim nodded.

He was still there an hour later when Dick packed his briefcase and returned to the Royal Imperial. He dined in his room after chatting virtually non-stop to Mary for an hour and 'unloading' on her. Being the good journalist she was she wanted to know all the details. The more she knew, the better the advice she would be able to give him in the weeks ahead.

CHAPTER SIX

Dick was in the office by 8.05 on Wednesday morning. This time he didn't have it to himself because he could tell by the smell and the noise that the kitchen was being put to good use. He took the set of keys he had been given two days ago and found one which locked all the drawers in the sideboard and another which locked the bulging filing cabinet. He made enough free space in the former to use when needed because he was determined not to leave one scrap of paper on any table when he was out of the office. He was certain somebody would be keen to know what his plans were. Exactly who, he would find out in due course.

There was no nine o'clock rush. He saw only one reporter dash in late and that by just a few minutes. He could live with that. At 9.05 he walked through both the advertising and editorial departments and as far as he could see everybody was doing something. Whether it was productive was another matter, but Lulu Popplewell was obviously chasing them up to sell the advertising space still available in each title that week.

"It's your monthly bonus that's at stake," he heard her tell one woman.

Nobody acknowledged his presence in either department. Only Edna Sparrow grappling with a mountain of post looked up and in the process dropped several letters on the floor.

Tim Fletcher was in his editor's office more than an hour earlier than the day before. Dick knew he should not take up too much of his time on what should be an important day editing that Friday's paper, but some things could not wait.

"I want you or one of your reporters to arrange a meeting for me and you on Monday afternoon in the boardroom with the deaconess and her friend. I understand from last week's Herald they are now living together not far away. I would like to have a friendly chat with them in the hope they might be able to provide us with something of a defence should this unfortunate matter ever go to court. You can deal with the Press Council, but keep me fully informed.

Tim gave him no more than his now customary nod. He was finding it very difficult to say anything meaningful to this imposing man.

Dick was satisfied with the limited response, but had not yet finished what he had come to say.

"I hope to meet the other two editors when they arrive today to put their papers to bed. I shall be telling them the same as I am going to tell you – as from Monday morning every reporter will look a lot smarter than they currently do. They represent the company to the public, so in future the men will wear ties and I don't mean something which looks like a piece of string. They can wear jumpers over the tops of their shirts, but a tie must be clearly visible. I do hope they all own a jacket."

Tim was about to say something at last, but then thought better of it.

"I am not going to carry out regular inspections, but if anyone looks unsuitably dressed they will be given one warning only. Clean clothes which don't smell of food will be mandatory. If anybody wishes to complain or discuss what is acceptable or is not my door will always be open."

Dick realised this was the first of what he suspected would be several instructions he would be well advised to put in writing. When he returned to the haven of the boardroom he rang Margaret Evans and asked her to have a memo ready for him to sign on Friday so he could send it out to all concerned next week. He dictated a second one about the rules governing breakfasts in the canteen he would post on the four notice boards just to be on the safe side.

He heard Margaret chuckle.

"Is it really that bad in Broad Bottom?" she asked.

"Much, much worse," he replied.

He had a lot of reading to do in addition to the first notes Edna Sparrow had typed up from the reporters' notebooks. The filing cabinet contained minutes of previous management and board meetings, four years of weekly trading reports and countless other papers. He would have to decide in due course what to keep and what he should take to Torchester and have shredded under Margaret's watchful eye.

He was surprised to discover that until recently, and despite his age, Harvey Fairbanks had insisted on sorting the post every morning. He was not averse to opening anything which dropped through the letterbox even when it was addressed to a named person and marked personal. Dick could only wonder as to what Harvey expected to discover.

It was while he was munching on a ham and tomato sandwich that a knock on the boardroom door heralded the arrival of Ellen McCraken and Adrian Wall, the two editors he had yet to meet. He ushered them in and realising they were probably just as hungry as he was told them it was alright for them to open their lunch boxes. He popped his head out into reception and got one of the girls to make a pot of coffee.

He could tell they were on their guard. One thing which he guessed had quickly been fed back to the other offices within the newspaper group was information about yesterday's goings on at the Broad Bottom Herald Express. *The telephone lines must have been red hot*, he thought as the two editors filed in. Neither of them attempted to sit down until they were invited to.

"You might be relieved to hear that I know very little about both of you," Dick said with a smile creeping across his face.

"As far as I am concerned everybody starts with a clean slate so why don't you give me a personal potted history over a cup of coffee after you have had something to eat."

Ellen was first to react. She brought out a box which appeared to contain a variety of leaves and other bits along with two pieces of bread which definitely didn't come from a sliced loaf.

Adrian's lunch was the more traditional – a sandwich with some filling, a chunk of cucumber and some grapes.

Thank goodness there was no marmite, thought Dick. If there was one thing he could not stand it was the smell of marmite.

He was not surprised to learn Ellen was Scottish – with a name like McCraken he would have been amazed if she had been born anywhere else. She told him she had followed her husband to Cornwall when he was head-hunted by a local high-tech electronics firm and had been fortunate enough to arrive at the same time the former editor of the Crackington by Sea Gazette and Piddle Wood Times had retired. She had started as a junior reporter on the Oban Times and worked her way up the editorial ladder. On the surface she appeared confident in her own abilities, thought Dick.

Adrian had been recruited in a local wine bar while on holiday in the area five years ago. He enjoyed fishing. He had moved from Worcester where he had been a sub-editor on Berrow's Journal, reputedly the world's oldest weekly newspaper. The move had enabled him to indulge his hobby while editing the smallest two papers in the group – the Tinkerbush News and Upperthong Observer. He said he liked his work, thought he had a good team of reporters and sub-editors and was sorry when Harvey Fairbanks sold the business 'because he enjoyed a good day out with him catching a variety of fish along the coast.'

For the first time since he had set foot in Cornwall Dick actually enjoyed a chat with two locals. He quizzed both of them carefully about how they ran their offices, but could not detect anything that should worry him. He passed on to them the instruction with regard to the company's future dress code policy, but both said it would not be a problem in their offices because they had always agreed reporters had to look the part when out and about.

Ellen gave him a knowing look when he mentioned the kitchen.

"Long overdue," was her opinion. "I had to make it quite clear to my team that breakfast was something you ate at home or on your way to work, but not at work. If I ever had to come into this office first thing in the morning I used to hate the smell on my clothes when I left."

Dick felt he had at least one person he might be able to confide in should it be necessary during what he hoped would be no more than a short term stay. He would make a point of visiting their respective offices next week, as long as the lawyers did not take up too much of his time. The two editors left together.

Thankfully, the rest of his afternoon was quiet. He fielded several phone calls from his Essex editors with regard to staff appointments and made a quick one of his own to Mary who was signing off the pages of her own paper in the Torchester printworks to check she was ok. She, too, was having a busy week because yesterday two college students had taken a dinghy from Thurnham harbour and crashed it on rocks. One had died from multiple injuries after having most of his left leg chopped off by a propeller, while the other had drowned. His body had been washed up on a nearby beach that morning. One of Mary's reporters had managed to interview the two women who had found the body while out for an early morning walk. It must not have been a pretty sight.

It had been a rush but Mary and her deputy had managed to beat the noon deadline and get the full story on pages one and three.

He missed her, but he did not allow himself to dwell too long on how he wished he was going to see her that evening because he knew he would become morose, and that would not do or solve the problems he felt were piling up.

For the next hour he read the minutes of the last two years' monthly board meetings, carefully noting anything which he felt he ought to know about the way the business was run. He soon discovered reporting procedures were much slacker than those employed by the Thompson Group – Jack Wilde would want that to change very quickly. Lulu Popplewell's reports were the most informative which gave him some hope that the commercial figures the sale of the company had been based on were correct.

There wasn't a financial department as such – this had been outsourced several years ago. The file Jack Wilde had given him last week said he did not need to bother himself with that side of things. He knew that in time the finance department would be moved in-house.

Thank heaven for small mercies, thought Dick.

The monthly reports submitted by Tim Fletcher and Frank Helliwell said very little of note. The circulation manager did not attend board meetings unless requested, but he and his small team appeared to have good relationships with their newsagents and the national Newsagents Federation. He would introduce himself when the opportunity arose, but unless any problem was flagged up he didn't expect to make any major decisions with regard to that department. He had more than enough to worry about without interfering with a system which appeared to be well run.

Elsewhere in the Herald Express office people were not quite as relaxed. Tim Fletcher did not usually arrange any tennis lessons or club business for Wednesdays. He knew he had to be in the office all day as the final stories were placed on the last nine pages which had to be completed by early evening. It was not unusual most weeks for last-minute adverts to be sold which meant his editorial team had to re-do some pages on a Wednesday evening or early Thursday morning. While his able deputy, Claire Burton, covered for him most days when he was out of the office, there were limits.

Lulu Popplewell placed late adverts on two pages just before five o'clock, but what worried Tim was the lack of a really good page one splash. He left his office and berated chief reporter Tony Morrisey in front of the others. He couldn't stop himself, although he knew it was not the way to get the best out of people.

"We have three hours to come up with something better than a report which reveals the council is failing to repair its housing stock. Ideally, I would like something that might cheer up our readers, but if that is beyond you a good old fashioned tragic accident on the ring road will do."

He knew who he would like to be in the car – somebody currently sitting in the boardroom.

When the editor returned to his office Tony in turn rounded on the six reporters. It was the way it had always been done at the Herald – pass it down the line.

"You had better buck up your ideas if you want a future in journalism because I think our new editorial director will go through each paper with a fine toothcomb from now on and will ask plenty of questions about the way we operate. Don't say you have not been warned."

They simply stared at him and when they were certain he had finished dropped their heads and continued working on their last stories for this particular edition. None of them offered to chase up anything better than they already had. They did what they were given, but didn't appear to have an original thought between them.

Edna Sparrow knew that she at least did her job well. Nobody ever had cause to shout at her – even if they dared. She was the office 'aunty' who covered all angles. When she was on holiday it was the nearest thing to total chaos in the office. She handled all stationery requests, collated reporters' and photographers' expenses for Tim to sign each Friday, managed the office petty cash, kept the absentee list, provided first aid when anyone cut themselves, typed up readers' letters and handled all Tim's internal and external correspondence. She also managed the one list Harvey Fairbanks had never seen and at all costs she had to keep well away from Mr Chinnery.

She had already sensed how within two days the man from head office had changed the atmosphere in the building. She had spent most of today sending stuff by fax or registered post to Richard Orange at Root's and typing up the final shorthand notes provided by the two reporters who between them had done the deaconess stories. Their shorthand was a joke. How they expected to reach 100 words a minute and take their exams was beyond her. They had had enough lessons, all paid for by the company, but she knew from her own secretarial training at night school that attaining the necessary shorthand speed needed hard work and dedication. They were in short supply at the Herald Express.

Rufus Jones did just enough each day to justify his existence. Or so he thought. He had not touched the deaconess story even though he was the most experienced reporter in this particular office, if not the group. He did not mind being handed a stack of press releases each week and being asked to turn them into stories which were readable if not very interesting. It was an easy life. He found court reporting more arduous and positively hated attending parish council meetings. He was not a member of staff as such, preferring to be treated as a freelance who submitted a weekly invoice. He worked Tuesday morning to Thursday tea-time and had been given some freedom with regard to his most creative work of the week – his expenses sheet. He was the late reporter Dick had spotted that morning and was clever enough to recognise he would have to be more careful in future.

Three times a day he got up from his desk to 'exercise my dodgy hip'. It was his excuse to walk through to the production department, not to see the news pages up on the boards but the classified adverts – the small ads as they were called - most of them free to people wanting to sell all manner of items. He was on the lookout for the real bargains which could earn him some money on the side. He had been surprised how lucrative it had become given that he had a minimum 24 hour start on anyone who bought the paper. A couple of times he had been spotted making notes and taking down telephone numbers, but nobody had said anything, because they had their own money-making operation to protect. Rufus knew that a word in the wrong ear about that would cause mayhem.

Dick deliberately left everyone to their own devices that second afternoon. Tim Fletcher came in to tell him their meeting with the deaconess and her 'girlfriend' had been fixed for 3pm on Monday.

"I definitely want you there – no excuses," he was told. "Ask Edna to raid petty cash and buy some nice chocolate biscuits because I think we could be in for a long session."

Inwardly Tim groaned, yet again. At this rate he would soon have an ulcer. That put an end to his Monday afternoon tennis lessons – his cold had just got a lot worse!

Lulu Popplewell was the only other person who interrupted Dick. She said she was delighted to tell him they had sold a goodly number of last-minute adverts today. He offered his congratulations, but her smile fell away when he asked how much they had been discounted from the normal rate.

"We got about 50% of the rate card for most of them," she said.

"Let's talk about that soon, Lulu, because I suspect some of your crafty businesses are holding on until the last minute to place their adverts in the knowledge they might snap up a bargain as you hurry to fill the paper. Yields are something my boss is very keen on."

She had to admit he had a point.

Dick avoided the five o'clock rush, but did not stay late in the office. He was tired and needed to take a break and do some thinking. That night he slept well after reading a couple of chapters of a book he had brought with him and after a good breakfast he booked a room at the Royal Imperial for the next three weeks. He hoped he would not be needed for any longer. Much would depend on who Henry Thompson and Jack Wilde appointed as the Herald Express's new managing director.

Thursday was the busiest day of the week for the production team and press crew. Editor and advertising manager signed off pages at regular intervals, while individual reporters and advertising reps wandered backwards and forwards to see if their work had been correctly handled. Dick was pleased to see that Lulu insisted she was given proofs of the main adverts so her team could correct any errors and hopefully reduce the number of expensive credit notes which had to be given to clients when their advertising was messed up. As far as he could see she ran a good department and worked hard. He had liked the way she had reacted to the criticism he had levelled the night before about discounted advertising. Rather than sulk she had taken on board what he had told her.

Before he left to begin the long drive to Essex, he told both of them he would be in Torchester tomorrow and gave them his telephone number along with that of his secretary.

"Tim, I want you to ring me with anything you hear from the solicitors or the Press Council. Please arrange for a copy of every paper to be left in the boardroom to await my return. I will see you on Monday; in the meantime remind your reporters about the new dress code and have a good weekend."

And with that he was gone. The Broad Bottom Herald Express had never seen anything like it. But there was much more to come.

CHAPTER SEVEN

He was grateful that once out of Cornwall and onto the M5 at Exeter the trip home via Bristol and then almost the entire length of the English part of the M4 to the M25 round London was event-free, much as Jack had predicted. Dick had had enough excitement for one week. The nearer he got to Thurnham, the better he felt.

When he pulled into their drive he saw that Mary was already home. He opened the front door and the smell from the kitchen told him she had made his favourite meal – steak and kidney pie with new potatoes followed by apple pie and custard. She gave him a long lingering kiss and then patted his stomach.

"This is a one-off Mr Husband because I bet you have had a cooked breakfast most days while you have been away and I am not going to have you putting on too much weight."

He hugged her until she broke free to attend to her cooking. Afterwards they snuggled up on the sofa to watch Doctor Who followed by the Terry Wogan Show, during which Dick fell asleep.

The following morning both of them were up early. Mary left home before him to visit her High Street office and do some initial planning for the following week's Thurnham and Shaldon Standard.

Dick felt sluggish but after a shower he was ready for what he hoped would be an easier day. Within an hour he had collected his wife from the Standard and together they travelled the 20 miles to head office in plenty of time for the editors' meeting. He reflected on how good it felt to be back on familiar territory with people he trusted and he knew excelled at their jobs.

Jack Wilde had left an agenda which Dick scanned for any potential troublesome items. There weren't any. Each editor had submitted a written report; they were taken as read so as not to waste time, unless anyone had any questions. The meeting progressed smoothly. There was a reminder to keep within budget and a presentation by the finance director on possible capital expenditure to upgrade two of the offices. The final item before any other business was down to him to report on his trip to Cornwall – they had eventually been told the day before where he was. He gave them another of those looks his editors had come to recognise in recent years and then let rip with all that had happened. The only interruptions came when they burst out laughing or ribbed him a little.

"I suppose some of you have been doing your own investigating to ensure I have not been sat in a deckchair on some Cornish beach," he joked. "But let me warn you that if any of you misbehave while I am away you will be sent by public transport to Cornwall to cover for me while I take a few days off. Believe me you will think you have been sent to the end of the earth."

One editor produced a straw hat and handed it over.

"We thought you might need that next week," he said. "We had a whip round. We can't have you not looking the part."

And on that note Dick closed the meeting.

Mary stayed behind for a few minutes. She took the straw hat off him.

"You know what editors are like," she said. "As soon as they knew where you had gone, they did some checking up, but not on you, silly. They know you have taken on quite a task with some difficult people. If you need any help in the south west all of them, including me, will volunteer to help if it gets nasty, even if it means travelling by public transport"

He kissed her then let her go as she had a train to catch back to Thurnham.

"Just remember to be fair as well as tough," were her parting words.

When she disappeared out of sight he went to see his secretary to catch up on anything she felt only he should handle. There wasn't much. Jack Wilde came back as promised by mid afternoon and didn't detain him long. They mainly chatted about the Ryan Johnston legal threat and Dick's gut feeling there was much more to some of the things he had heard or seen while in Broad Bottom than he yet realised.

Less than five miles away from where the editors were meeting Deputy Chief Constable Johnston was in a far less happy mood. It had been a good week until yesterday when his secretary had brought in a copy of that night's Torchester Evening Gazette. The front page had carried a picture of both him and his wife – to his disgust it showed him in uniform. There for all to see laid bare had been the current state of his marriage. Now he knew why that reporter had tried hard to speak to him, but had failed to track him down when he was in the House of Commons and elsewhere in London.

Dick Chinnery's telephone call to the Gazette's editor on Tuesday had resulted in a well written factually correct story, but, unlike what had appeared in recent editions of the Broad Bottom Herald Express, there was nothing that the Deputy Chief Constable could legally challenge. And to make matters worse there were several unhelpful personal comments from close family, including that busybody aunt of his wife's. *She should stick to selling her garden produce*, he thought.

He had known all too well the damage this could do to his career. He had had no choice but to ask for an immediate meeting with Keith Wood, the Chief Constable, where he had brazened it out. It had not been pleasant, but it could have been worse. His boss had strict moral values, did not drink, believed in family life as the strength of the nation and expected his team to follow his example. He had recently engineered the removal of two of his senior officers who had had affairs with other policemen's wives. His views on lesbian relationships could only be imagined. He took any critical coverage in the media seriously. As far as he was concerned anybody who did anything to undermine his force didn't have a future.

Until now Ryan Johnston had not told anyone within the force about his proposed legal action against the Cornish newspaper. He had hoped the distance between the two would be sufficient to keep the matter a private one. He had been told by his expensive London solicitors that on an initial examination he had a very winnable case for an action for damages and that in most such cases the newspaper concerned coughed up the money and paid the defamed person's legal bill before it ever got anywhere near a court room. He confidently expected the matter to be resolved within a few weeks and his bank account to be healthier.

But now the story was out locally it was a different matter. He had told the Chief Constable the full story about his private life - his version at least – and about the separation from his wife Annabel. He had been relieved to discover that the fact he had already taken decisive legal action was a point in his favour as far as his old fashioned boss was concerned.

"Get a settlement in your favour and get it sorted in double quick time," had been the Chief Constable's only advice. "I presume you have told me everything?"

Ryan Johnston confirmed he had with a nod of his head. There would be a time and a place to introduce everyone to the new love in his life, but this wasn't it. He had been relieved when he had been dismissed.

On his way into his office at County Police HQ today he thought he had heard somebody talking about him at the far end of a long corridor.

"What sort of a man forces his wife to run off with another woman?" was the only complete sentence he could say for definite he had heard correctly.

He did not know the people concerned and they had moved on quickly before he could challenge them. By the time he had reached the end of the corridor and turned left there had been nobody in sight.

For the rest of the morning he could not concentrate on the weekly reports on his desk. He knew it was no good dwelling on something he could do nothing about, but all the same he yearned for the soothing words of Marie-Clementine, plus the other comforts she would bring. Thank goodness it was Friday.

CHAPTER EIGHT

No news was good news as far as Dick was concerned. On Friday afternoon he resisted the temptation to ring Tim Fletcher or Lulu Popplewell before he left his office, gave his secretary a peck on the cheek and went home. He was determined to try and enjoy his weekend and have a couple of relaxing days he felt he needed to clear his head. He could not totally forget the Broad Bottom Herald Express, though.

He took Mary out to dinner in Thurnham on Friday night at a select back street restaurant near the water's edge and got a kick under the table when she realised he was not listening fully to what she was telling him about what she had been doing all week. She changed tack and did what she always did best – she made him laugh about his work.

"From what you have told me there are some strange characters doing all sorts of unusual things at this newspaper group, so why don't we compare them with some of the other strange people you and I have known?"

"Anyone in particular you have in mind?" he quipped.

"Nothing will ever beat that deputy editor changing sex over the weekend," she said. "He was Andy on Friday and Jessica on Monday. Remember all the problems you had with the rest of the staff who didn't want him/her in their toilets?"

How could he ever forget? He had eventually solved that problem by providing 'Jessica' with a key to the boardroom toilet. The print unions had been awkward too; they had warned they would walkout if a man dressed as a woman came into their domain.

"What about that reporter who came to work in smelly clothes and rarely seemed to wash?" she asked.

That had been another unpleasant experience. Two people had complained that sitting in the same room as him most days made them feel sick. The reporter had ignored repeated warnings about his appearance and had eventually been dismissed. When he took the case to an industrial tribunal the company won an important ruling.

"Right, it's your turn now," said Dick. "What's the funniest situation you have had to handle when dealing with staff?"

Mary took her time before replying.

"I think it has to be the Saturday afternoon I called in at the Standard to collect some papers and found two of my reporters stark naked on my large desk. You should have seen their faces! They told me they had only come into the office to do their expenses sheets."

Dick remembered the story well. He was the only other person who knew what had occurred, his wife having taken the sensible, in his opinion, decision that it really was nothing to do with her if two single people had some fun at the weekend – although she had drawn the line at her office ever being used again.

"I think we ought to write down all these stories and others we can remember for posterity," suggested Dick. "I have a feeling the Herald Express will provide us with many more before I am finished."

On Saturday afternoon they went to see the latest Bond film A View to a Kill starring Roger Moore and later shared the sofa to watch Match of the Day. She often feigned interest in football, but he wasn't fooled. He had received another painful dig in the ribs one Saturday night when he had asked her to explain the offside rule.

Sunday was taken up with a long morning walk along the sea front, past the Thames barges moored at Thurnham quayside, and a late roast lunch which included a bottle of red wine they had finished off between them.

Both of them were ready for an early night after he had packed his suitcase ready for the week ahead. Mary made sure he had a clean shirt for every day, a second suit and a variety of ties to compliment his favourite dark suit. She was determined her man would look the part for whatever tasks lay ahead - the following morning she was equally determined to drive him to Stansted airport for his very early flight.

Dick arrived at St Mawgan at 7.30 and was in his boardroom office 50 minutes later for what he felt would be another interesting but mentally tiring week. The first thing he did was to check the lock on the sideboard to make sure it had not been tampered with. It was untouched.

On the boardroom table was a pile of last week's papers for him to study, a complete personnel list, courtesy of Edna Sparrow, Frank Helliwell and Lulu Popplewell and several weekly reports from editors and advertising managers. The list he was most interested in was the 'sick' report. He opened the sideboard and eventually found several years' reports which he studied for the next hour over his first coffee of the day. He had a gut feeling that he would find something interesting and he was not disappointed. Just about every week at least two, and often three, of the press crew did not turn up for work on a Tuesday. The only exceptions to this pattern were round Christmas and Easter.

He thought it was time he met them. He meandered his way through the advertising department and into the more familiar sounding newsroom with its clickity-clack of typewriters, where several reporters with their heads down appeared to be immersed in their work.

He would not have noticed the challenge to his authority if someone had not smirked and made him look around. Two of the reporters, like their colleagues, had obeyed his instruction to wear a tie. One was vivid yellow and contained what looked like gravy stains, while the other featured a rude sexual innuendo above which appeared to be a naked woman.

The press crew would have to wait.

He entered the editor's office without knocking and remained standing.

"Ask your chief reporter to join us," he ordered Tim Fletcher.

When Tony Morrisey arrived Dick didn't explode, but his tone was icy.

"Let me make another thing crystal clear: I hold both of you personally responsible for the behaviour of any member of your team. I assume you have seen this morning's childish reaction to my dress code edict by two of your reporters?"

Tony shrugged his shoulders. Neither of them commented. It was probably a wise decision.

"If anyone, and I stress anyone, thinks they can undermine any manager's authority – particularly mine - in this company they will be looking for a new job in record time. I won't ask why you didn't do something about it before I saw the way two people under your command had dressed for work. Call the pair of them in."

Tony retreated and came back with two grinning reporters a few minutes later.

Dick did not give them any chance to speak before he launched into the offensive while standing directly in front of them.

"So you think your appearance today is good enough for you to represent the company at a Chamber of Commerce press conference do you, or interview somebody in their home?"

"Can't you take a joke?" muttered the older one.

It was an unwise comment. Dick took his time.

"I have the intelligence to understand the difference between a joke and something totally different. Let me tell you something funny."

There was silence.

"I have just had a look at the company's personnel files and it seems that reporters are only on two weeks' notice. It seems Harvey Fairbanks didn't pay much attention to such matters when he owned the company. There are hundreds of youngsters coming off university and college journalism courses who cannot find work – they would love the opportunity to sit at your desks."

He had their full attention now. The younger reporter looked pale.

"You have an hour to go back home and find more suitable attire. If you do not want to adhere to the company dress code and would prefer not to return to work please have the good manners to telephone Tim and I will arrange for you to be paid off. And while you are at it you can, with my permission, tell everyone in the next room what has just happened – I would not like to have to repeat this conversation to anyone else."

And with that he was gone. It was time to talk to the press crew and get some answers from them. He felt energised for whatever lay ahead.

*

Frank Helliwell's greeting was just as hearty as it had been the previous Tuesday. Dick, however, was not in the mood for very much small talk after his altercation in the news room; he asked Frank to introduce him to the press crew and after a few preliminaries got straight to the point.

"You look as though you have your hands full on Wednesdays and Thursdays, but apart from printing the Herald Express on a Monday evening you appear to have a lot of spare capacity."

The looks Frank and the press crew exchanged did not go unnoticed.

Dick decided some bluff was called for.

"We will be looking to bring in some extra work because as you know a printing press needs to keep running as many hours as possible to make it viable. Tuesday looks a promising day if we can win a contract."

One small stocky man could not stop himself from blurting out:" You can't do that."

It was the opening Dick had hoped he would get.

"And why not, may I ask?"

"Because, because .... well we do maintenance, cleaning and other things every Tuesday. A printing press needs careful handling."

Dick turned on his most gracious smile

"Printing the Herald Express on a Monday evening must make you all sick."

They looked at him non-plussed.

"From what I can make out some of you cannot face the world the next day and regularly report in sick. It must be really hard work for those who do turn up and have all that maintenance and cleaning to do with half a team."

There was no response. Dick didn't want to press home his advantage just yet.

"I will keep you informed but you might get a visit from the Torchester production director later this month. I will try to ensure it is not on a Tuesday."

And with that he left them as quickly as he had left the editorial department. On his way back to the board room he repeated over and over again his old football quips: two-nil, two-nil, two-nil. He felt better.

Frank Helliwell stayed behind to field what he knew would be the worried press crew's inevitable questions. He had no answers as to what they should do next, but he assured them that he would keep them informed of any developments. He tried not to sound worried - but he was. He needed to speak to Edna Sparrow at the first opportunity.

CHAPTER NINE

Dick spotted his two mid-afternoon guests as soon as they drove into the car park. Shortly after, there was a knock on the boardroom door and they walked into his office, followed by Tim Fletcher who had arranged for his secretary to prepare two pots of coffee. She had spread a liberal number of chocolate biscuits onto two plates.

"Would you like me to take some minutes?" enquired Edna Sparrow when she had finished bringing in the coffee.

"I don't think so, but thank you for asking," Dick replied.

She shut the door behind her and returned to her desk to cover for Tim's absence.

The Herald's editor did the introductions while Dick poured the coffee. Mrs Annabel Johnston took hers black, while Miss Brea Williams liked milk and two sugars; Tim had milk and one sugar, he noted.

"I want to thank you for agreeing to this meeting so quickly," Dick began. "I think you ought to see the letter we have had from Mr Johnston's solicitors in London before we go any further."

He passed over copies for both of them to read.

"A damn cheek," remarked Mrs Johnston. "A damn cheek."

And before he could stop her she launched into a long indictment of her husband. Dick only interrupted her to clarify a couple of points. When she had finished, for the time being at least, he asked the one question the answer to which he had to be sure about before they proceeded any further.

"As far as you are both concerned the stories the Herald Express has carried are true and you are prepared to say so to our solicitors?"

"Without a doubt, they are true," said Miss Williams. "We have nothing but praise for the tactful way two of your reporters interviewed us, checked the main facts before publication and quoted us accurately."

Be thankful for small mercies, thought Dick; *it is a pity they don't know much about the libel laws!*

"As you can see from Mr Johnston's letter he is claiming that he has never had an affair at any time during his marriage and is not currently living with a French woman. What evidence can you show me that might help to stop this legal action before it gets expensive for us?"

"I am sure several members of the family will be willing to provide written statements about his behaviour," replied the policeman's wife.

They might be inadmissible in law, thought Dick.

He chatted to them for more than half an hour while Tim stayed tight-lipped.

Dick had no reason to doubt they were telling him the truth, indeed he warmed to both of them as the meeting progressed, but as to actual evidence that would stand up in a court of law, he was sceptical.

The meeting appeared to have come to a natural end when from the shopping bag she had brought with her Mrs Johnston put a folder in front of him. She looked him straight in the eye.

"My husband thinks he is being clever as well as greedy," Mr Chinnery, "but before I left Chelmsford I discovered these in his bedroom drawer. When you have read the documents and letters in that folder you might feel they are useful in your attempts to persuade him to back off and forget any thoughts of taking you to court."

She gave him the most knowing of smiles.

Dick took hold of the folder before Tim Fletcher could move. He would read its contents on his own.

Both women stood up to indicate they felt they had said and done enough for the moment. They shook his hand which forced Tim to stand up too and show them out to the car park via the reception area. When the Herald editor returned Dick did not give him the chance to ask what was in the folder.

"I am sure you have plenty of catching to do in the news room, so I won't detain you any longer," Dick told him.

Tim had the good sense to realise he had been dismissed.

Dick made himself a cup of tea, grabbed two biscuits and opened the folder.

At first he didn't fully understand the importance of what he was reading, but he knew correspondence between a senior policeman - with obvious political connections in London – and several Eastern European embassies was way above anything he had ever dealt with. It made his fight six years ago to expose corruption in Thurnham appear tame by comparison.

He was keen to fax the entire folder's contents to Richard Orange there and then to get an expert legal opinion on such sensitive and potentially explosive material now in his possession, but when he phoned his London lawyer's office he discovered he was not expected to return that afternoon. Dick realised he had no choice but to telephone him at home that evening and then get into the office early next morning before anyone else could see what he was doing.

He wanted to be sure each letter and document was viewed only by a select few people. What their lawyer would make of them was anybody's guess. He feared there would be some searching questions about how he came to be in possession of such private and politically sensitive items.

Dick waited until the majority of the Herald Express's staff had left, Tim included, before ringing Jack Wilde. His managing director was not prone to expressing too many feelings but even he whistled when Dick began to tell him what he had in his possession.

"You certainly like to swim in the deep end," he exclaimed. "Make two copies of what you have and keep them in separate locations. Tomorrow I shall send a courier to collect one copy which I will read and keep safely here in Torchester. Lock another copy in the boardroom and keep the original in your locked briefcase until you return to Essex."

It was good advice. He found the keys for the pool car Tim Fletcher had left him and went back to the Royal Imperial Hotel from where he rang his wife.

"How has your day gone?" was Mary's first question.

"Oh, fairly quiet really; you know what it is like down here" he replied sardonically.

"Liar, liar, house on fire," she yelled back.

She knew him too well to be fooled.

"Is it that bad you can't tell me over the phone?"

"I am afraid so."

There was a pause before she said:" Then come home soon and tell me all about it then."

It was the right answer. For the next 20 minutes she told him about the stories she had been handling including one about the release from prison of a certain Toby Walters, ex estate agent.

Dick was not happy that the man who had assaulted his wife was back on the streets of Thurnham and he was 350 miles away.

She also had a page one splash she knew would sell extra papers about the sacking of Radio Thurnham's long standing lunch-time presenter. He had been shown the door after refusing to make changes to a programme which delighted anyone aged over 60, but failed to interest key advertisers upon whom the station depended. They wanted programmes which drew a younger and middle-aged audience – housewives and people in their cars.

"What a shame. No more Val Doonican or Des O'Connor records then. Whatever will I do?" said Dick.

"I hear Mr Walters is going into the used car business," added Mary. "I bet we don't get his advertising!"

Dick laughed along with her, but he knew that underneath she would be just as concerned as he was about the return of Mr Walters to Thurnham. He only hoped the former estate agent cum mason had had enough of prison not to seek any sort of revenge.

When he reluctantly put the phone down on her he made three more calls and then eventually found Richard Orange at home. The normally reserved lawyer gave vent to a rare show of emotion when Dick revealed what Mrs Johnston had handed over.

After briefing him and agreeing that they would both go to their offices early tomorrow, Dick re-read the documents. The longer he studied them the more he understood what he had in his possession. Afterwards he was too pre-occupied and single-minded to want to engage anyone in conversation in the hotel dining room, so he ate in his room, watched some television and even read a little before slipping between the sheets. But sleep did not come easy. And it was still only Monday.

CHAPTER TEN

He woke early, far too early, his mind racing - he knew there was no point in trying to get back to sleep. After a continental breakfast in his room Dick was out of the hotel by 7.20. It was a beautiful early summer's morning after yesterday's heavy rain. He could smell the sea air, but there was no time for him to take a walk. The office car park was empty and the building in semi darkness, which enabled him to enter the boardroom without anyone seeing him. He gave himself a mental pat on the back for writing down the alarm code which he had instantly forgotten when he had been given it last week.

It took a few minutes for the fax machine to start up. He prayed it would not take half an hour to send each item. Thankfully, it didn't.

At the other end Richard Orange waited. From what the lawyer already knew this was one job he could not trust to anyone, even his own secretary.

Several women carrying bags of food came into the Herald Express office soon after eight o'clock and went straight to the kitchen. They didn't bother him and he didn't bother them, that was until 9.02 when he deliberately popped in to wash out a cup. Three advertising reps and a reporter beat a hasty retreat.

He spent most of the morning waiting for Richard's phone call and reading last week's papers. He enjoyed flicking through Ellen McCraken's two papers; they were well written and contained a number of human interest stories he always liked to see in any local paper. She employed a couple of lively columnists, but he felt she needed to give her sports editor, who covered both titles, a bit of a kicking because there were too many missed words or poor spellings – a sure sign he was not checking carefully enough the match reports submitted by amateur correspondents.

He took a short walk through the building and discovered the 'sickness bug' had struck the press room yet again. Today was not the day to tackle that problem, but he knew he could not put it off for too long.

It was Lulu Popplewell who broke the peace in his office early in the afternoon after, much to his surprise, he had enjoyed a short nap.

"I think I ought to ask for your opinion on this," she said as she sat down in front of him. "One of the most popular features in five of our papers is the free ads when readers can sell anything they want as long as it is priced under £100. We don't carry them in Tuesday's Herald Express because we want to build up the circulation of the Friday paper."

It made sense to Dick. They did something similar with the evening paper in Torchester.

"I have just spoken to one reader/advertiser who wanted to know how come she had received four phone calls last Wednesday evening about various items she was selling before the paper was on sale on Friday? It is not the first time somebody has complained about that happening to them, but it is the first time I have been given the name of the buyer."

Dick knew another problem was about to rear its head.

"Who is responsible?" he asked.

"A certain Rufus Jones who sits in the editorial department three days a week and gives me the creeps every time he looks at me in a certain way."

He had not spoken to Rufus Jones last week; indeed, it seemed that the reporter had had his head down working hard every time Dick passed through. *Some people have the ability to look busy and produce nothing*, he thought.

"It's a grave breach of trust," added Lulu. "We cannot have our own staff taking advantage of their position. I suspect he buys items cheaply and sells them on at a profit. It doesn't cost him anything the following week to re-advertise the goods he bought the week before."

"Leave it with me," he told her, "but I need something in writing from you in the form of a memo."

She left to do it right away.

Dick got up and looked out of the window. *Just what else am I going to discover about these people and their ways* he mused, as he turned and marched off to see the Herald's editor. He was out. Edna Sparrow did not know where he could be contacted.

Dick fumed, but he was not going to be held up if he could help it. He got the editorial secretary to show him where the personnel files for the editorial department were kept - in the top drawer of Tim Fletcher's filing cabinet. He was not surprised they did not contain much apart from the barest of details on each staff member. Fortunately, it was enough.

He soon found what he wanted and took Rufus Jones' file back to the boardroom. He was pleased to discover that although Rufus was a freelance, he still came under the company's disciplinary code.

He wondered how Tim Fletcher would handle it.

Dick spotted the Herald editor an hour later when his dark blue Ford Escort pulled into the car park. He left the boardroom to meet up with him in reception.

"Just been out to chat to a good contact," Tim lied before Dick said anything.

"Next time please tell your secretary where you can be contacted," was Dick's chilly response. "What if we had had an emergency and you could not be found?"

Tim had the good sense to realise that his new editorial director had not come out to greet him to have a friendly chat.

"Something wrong?" he enquired.

"You better come in," replied Dick who spent the next 10 minutes spelling out how he expected the Herald's editor to handle Rufus Jones.

"I will deal with it later in the week," said Tim. "I am having a busy day one way and another."

Dick looked him in the eye. It was a look which had scared stronger characters than the Herald Express editor. It was enough to make Tim realise he had just given a man like Dick Chinnery the totally wrong response.

Tim suspected he was going to have another late departure from the office and there was absolutely nothing he would be able to do about it. His wife was not going to be happy, never mind the tennis club committee who were meeting at 7pm. *Thank goodness this awful man is only with us for short time*, he thought.

He left the boardroom after assuring Dick he would speak to his reporter right away.

*

At first Rufus Jones denied doing anything wrong when he stepped into the editor's office. "I am not the only person with that name in Cornwall," he angrily complained.

Edna Sparrow sat passively taking notes, but inwardly was enjoying seeing her unpopular colleague get caught out; she thought such a meeting was long overdue.

Tim, on the other hand, hated confrontation, but knew that if Rufus lied and tried to wiggle his way out of it, Dick Chinnery would have both of them on toast.

"For the record are you denying it is you, then?" he asked the reporter.

Rufus took a while to answer, but eventually said "no."

"Let me give you some of the best advice you will ever receive in this office. Own up to everything now, say sorry and promise that you won't do it again. You will get a written warning, but nothing more. If you try and brazen it out you could be out of work very soon and have a visit from the police."

"The police, why should they be involved?" spluttered Rufus.

"Because whichever way you look at it this is fraud, and who knows what an investigation might turn up. I bet some of your expenses claims would not stand up to much scrutiny if our new company's finance department had a look at them. And while I am at it, stop leering at the girls in advertising," added Tim.

It was the toughest he had ever been with any reporter. He was not enjoying the conversation one bit. If he had his way he would always do everything he could to avoid any sort of confrontation, including the simple expedient of hoping a problem would go away or solve itself. He had said enough though.

After a period of silence, Rufus capitulated, agreed to apologise and accepted the written warning. He realised he had little choice and left the room soon after.

Edna said nothing, but stored the information she had gleaned in the most important filing cabinet in the office – her brain.

Dick waited until six o'clock before going back to his hotel. He had not heard from either Richard Orange or Jack Wilde, but knew they would be in touch as soon as they had something to relay to him. He suspected Richard was working on a second letter to Deputy Chief Constable Ryan Johnston's solicitors. He would bet his entire savings it would be a 'stonker'.

*

Frank Helliwell and Edna Sparrow's business arrangement had benefited them and the six members of the press crew for nearly ten years; both felt it was now under threat after Harvey Fairbanks' rapid sale of the company. They had arranged to meet at the Red Lion in Piddle Wood on Tuesday evening for a 'council of war'.

"Do you think he knows what we are doing?" were Frank's opening words after he sat down with his pint of Whitbread. He was not used to feeling nervous.

"I have everything under lock and key in my filing cabinet, so you don't need to worry that he has found out anything from me," was Edna's terse reply, with enough emphasis on the 'me' to make her point.

Frank had no meant to suggest anything of the sort, but he felt the need to say something positive. He tried to offer her some reassurance.

"Printing contracts are not easy to obtain for Tuesdays", he uttered. "Companies want their newspapers printed as near as possible to the weekend so advertisers get the best response for their money unless a town has a midweek market."

Edna was not to be placated. She had seen enough already to know Dick Chinnery was nobody's fool and her private investigations had revealed he was like a dog with a bone when he got his teeth into something. She knew they needed a plan B.

"The men have come to rely on their monthly income from our scheme. Some of them have taken out hefty mortgages on the back of their extra earnings," Frank wittered on. "They won't give them up without a fight."

Edna instinctively knew it was a fight they could not hope to win if the full story came out. It was her job, it seemed, to do some thinking and ensure it never did.

"I don't think Mr Chinnery will be with us for that long. He has already indicated he is only in Broad Bottom for a few weeks to prepare a report for his board of directors. Let us see if we can ease his concerns about the missing men on a

Tuesday by ensuring everybody turns up for work for the next four weeks."

Frank was aghast.

"We will lose the contract."

Edna gave him one of her withering looks.

"We won't lose the contract, but we will do things a bit differently until we are rid of him. It is light early enough at this time of year for us to put in a couple of hours some mornings before we have to be at the Herald and it stays that way until quite late. Plus we have the weekends. I am sure our paymasters will understand and not be too bothered as long as they get what they want each week. Fix it. That's what you get paid for. You don't do much else"

She could see it had stung him that she could be so rude to his face, but he quickly recovered. He had heard her speak far more harshly to some of the reporters and even Tim Fletcher. He relaxed just a little and the beer tasted much better because of it. At least he would have some better news for his worried colleagues in the morning.

Edna was keen to leave, but when she stood up to put her coat on Frank indicated there was another matter he wished to discuss. She reluctantly sat down again.

"You may remember that when we set up this arrangement we agreed it would be equal shares for all - twelve and a half per cent of all revenues, minus costs, for each of us," he said. "We gave you an equal share because you were trusted to keep a good record of what we were due, arrange payment and quietly distribute it accordingly."

"So what's your problem?" she snapped back.

Frank took another mouthful of beer before telling her the rest of the team believed they had not been paid enough in recent months. She was not happy.

"You think I am fiddling you, do you?"

"Well some of the men have been checking the work they have done and it seems they believe that they are being short-changed."

She was furious. Heads turned to look at her as she stood up and gave him the strongest volley of abuse he and the other Red Lion regulars had heard for years.

"Tell your colleagues," she hissed, "that if any of them have enough brains to wade through my record keeping, invoices and bank statements they won't find a penny out of place. Somehow I doubt they would know where to start."

And with that she collected her coat, didn't bother to put it on and was gone. The screech of her car tyres could be heard soon after.

Frank thought she protested a bit too much, but her plan B was a good one.

*

In London that same evening Ryan Johnston met up with Marie-Clementine. He had hoped that by now his legal problems would have been concluded. His solicitor had just disabused him. They had received what everyone in legal circles knew was no more than a holding letter and although they had stressed the need to settle matters as soon as possible to 'stop the on-going damage to Ryan's reputation', it now seemed certain the newspaper would put up some sort of fight.

Only a few hours earlier the Deputy Chief Constable had received another piece of bad news. The Torchester Evening Gazette, being near to London, was far better read by a wider circle of people than any Cornish bi-weekly paper. His secretary had fielded a call from someone representing the satirical magazine Private Eye who wanted to ask him some pertinent questions about his love life. He knew if anything ever appeared in that journal his senior police career would be over. Worse, if any investigative reporter found out about the real aims of the luncheon club much, much worse would follow.

Marie-Clementine tried to calm him down. She was beginning to find his personal problems with his wife a distraction she could well do with out. However, she knew she needed him just as much as he needed her at this time.

"Until we know what we are dealing with there is no point in getting too worked up. Anyway we have enough friends in high places who can do us a few favours if need be."

He wasn't quite sure what she meant by that. He was beginning to realise there was much more to Marie-Clementine than he had first thought.

She was more focused on who they should invite to the next House of Commons lunch rather than some unimportant story about Ryan's lesbian wife in a local - to him - newspaper. She'd told him only a few hours earlier she'd been asked to arrange one more House of Commons get-together before several high-ranking people within the UK establishment and a leading member of the American administration would discover there was no such thing as a free lunch.

Her 'clients' had been delighted with the results from the last one, particularly Jurgen Weber and Sergei Mudkoi

CHAPTER ELEVEN

Wednesday morning was a waiting game for Dick. He knew Richard Orange would contact him when he had something useful to impart. He waited for the day to bring developments which gave him time to re-read the stories about the two women he had met yesterday. He felt it was a good story they had told about how they had 'fallen in love', but he was worried about whether the lack of real evidence concerning the extra marital affairs of the Deputy Chief Constable would be the Herald Express's undoing.

However, on the plus side the documents Mrs Johnston had left with him had revealed something potentially far more useful in the Herald's looming legal battle. But there was a possible catch: he pondered as to whether they could be sued for breach of privacy and confidentiality if they tried to use them as part of their defence. And while it was obvious that Ryan Johnston and his female French friend had a business arrangement, they could well argue it was exactly that. There was nothing illegal in two people of the opposite sex working together. The onus was on the Herald to prove the allegations they had made, not for Mr Johnston to disprove them.

He rang Jack Wilde in Torchester with a suggestion.

"Do you think it might be worth engaging the services for a couple of weeks of that private detective we have used before? He might be able to discover whether Mr Johnston and Miss Dubois are living together, or even photograph them hand in hand."

The managing director didn't see how it could do any harm.

"But it is a tad unusual to have a private detective trail a Deputy Chief Constable. Leave it with me to arrange, though, you have enough on your plate."

By late morning Dick had still not heard from Richard Orange. Tim Fletcher was his first visitor.

"I have dealt with Rufus Jones," he said, and then proceeded to give a quick resume of how the meeting had gone. "He owned up in the end but he is not very happy. I don't think he believes he has done anything really wrong and resents the written warning. I have no way of knowing how long it has been going on and it is probably not worth trawling past papers to check just how many of his own adverts he has placed after snapping up the best bargains cheaply. I would not put it past him, though, to try and find some way round the ban."

For once Dick agreed with the Herald's editor.

"In such cases, Tim, what always worries me is what don't we know about? OK, we have caught him out more by good luck than management, but what else is he up to – and for that matter what else is going on under our noses?"

Tim hoped his face did not show any reaction, but inside his heart was beating faster.

"I must get back because it is a busy day in the news room. I am hoping we have some better stories than last week."

And with that he was gone.

A strange man, thought Dick. But then this is Cornwall.

The news room was not a happy place. They knew the pressure was on to produce a good paper to impress both their temporary new boss and their new owners and several of them were still inwardly seething about the way they had been treated. One of their number, who played in a band in his spare time, kept muttering '*not earning enough bread at this game, man*'. Nobody took much notice.

The majority kept their hostile views to themselves, but Rufus Jones could not contain his anger. He bent the ear of anybody prepared to listen so within an hour that morning everybody knew what he was really up to when he wandered off each day, and the written warning.

The latter was something new at the Herald Express. In the past people had either left suddenly with no explanation or upped sticks and moved to another job elsewhere in the country. None of them had read the company's disciplinary rules.

Rufus got little sympathy from his colleagues who wanted to get on with their work with a deadline only a few hours away.

It was Edna Sparrow who eventually shut him up. Her ill mood had carried over from the night before.

"If you expect anybody to have any sympathy because you have been caught out cheating our readers," you are misguided she said. "You are lucky you still have a job because if it had been me I would have sacked you on the spot."

He started to protest, then thought better of it. However, he vowed not forget and hoped the time would come when he could settle the score with the unfriendly editorial secretary.

The two reporters who had made their silly protest over the tie policy also found Edna in an unforgiving mood. One had threatened to quit, but she had told him he was 'full of wind'. The other had enough financial problems without losing his job. Both now wore ties they had hastily bought on their way home last night. It had not helped their moods when their wives had laughed at them.

"It was about time somebody gave you a lesson in what constitutes reasonable work attire," she told them. "Harvey Fairbanks gets away with it because he is eccentric and in the main he is loved by people who forgive his funny ways. He is clueless when it comes to matching a red shirt with yellow trousers and blue socks, but that is part of his personality. All your clothes tell me is that you are grubby and have little self respect," she added.

Neither of them had an answer, although one muttered: "We will be lined up for inspection soon, clean shoes, crease in trousers, Windsor knot and the rest."

God help them if they ever try to get a job elsewhere, thought Edna, and left it at that. Nobody could ever say she did not look the part whether she was at work or elsewhere.

When Dick walked through the news room soon after lunch he spotted the new ties, but decided not to pass comment. In time he would ensure that when they were out in public all the reporters would be reasonably attired and present a good company image. He smiled at the thought of what Jack Wilde would say if he saw them - he would have a fit. He continued to the production area and spent half an hour reading some of the pages already finished - awaiting their turn in the photo processing room where the negatives were produced from which the plates which were strapped to the press were made.

Once again he found the Crackington by Sea Gazette the most engaging read of the four papers on display, even though he had no interest in its many parochial stories. He always thought that it was a good test of any newspaper if its stories persuaded him to read beyond the headlines and the front page.

On his travels he found both Ellen McCraken and Adrian Wall in a small side room which he thought was just about the most miserable looking room in the whole building – and it had some pretty stiff competition for that title. It had no windows and seemed to be full of stale air.

The two editors were sat side by side in front of a large desk which contained a mass of page proofs.

"It would be good to have a cup of tea with both of you this afternoon. What time might suit you?" he asked them.

Ellen replied on behalf of both of them. "I aim to be finished by three, but need to get away by four at the latest because I have a Rotary dinner to attend tonight and need to go home first to freshen up." Adrian said he would make it at the same time.

That suited Dick who returned to the boardroom, filled the kettle, set out a tray of cups and saucers and even found the rest of the chocolate biscuits. He did not think it fair to use Edna Sparrow as his tea lady too often.

When his phone rang he instinctively knew it was Richard Orange.

"Is it good news or bad?" he enquired.

"A mixed bag really," said Richard, who went on to suggest the future legal tactics they should employ.

"I am going to fax you a letter I would like to send to the Deputy Chief Constable in response to his threat to sue the Herald Express. I guess you don't want anyone else to see it so can I suggest you stand by your fax machine for a few minutes and take delivery?"

Dick obliged and spent the next fifteen minutes analysing the letter's contents before ringing Richard back.

"You have a lovely turn of phrase which sends a shiver down my back, even though I am not the one on the receiving end of your letters," said Dick.

"It's what I get paid for, old boy. I have to justify the invoices I send you. If Mr Johnston has any sense he will back off because the information provided by his wife is political and legal dynamite. She sounds a canny woman and we both know that a woman scorned etc etc ..."

Spot on thought, Dick.

"The bad news is I am not convinced we have any real evidence about the key part of his complaint, namely that he is shacked up with some French dolly bird, or that it is not the first time he has found his way into somebody else's bed," added the lawyer.

Dick decided to tell him about the private detective.

The lawyer thought it was a good idea. "Let's hope he comes up with something. At this stage there is no way I am going to let Mr Johnston or his lawyers see the documents in our possession. They will only be needed if the case ever goes to court. I think this letter should leave him in no doubt we have some pretty damning material; that should worry him no end."

Dick needed to clarify one other matter.

"Given what you have read and the fact I believe Mrs Johnston has even more information than she has shown us, do you think we should go to the police?"

There was a pause at the other end of the line.

"At some stage the answer is probably yes," Richard Orange replied, "but for the time being we will keep our powder dry. Senior police officers have friends within any force who conveniently have a habit of losing things. We would not want that to happen to Mrs Johnston's documents, would we?"

They spent another five minutes discussing the letter before Dick gave his go-ahead for it to be hand delivered later that afternoon. They were agreed the response when it came would be very interesting.

He had hardly put the phone down before Ellen and Adrian popped in to have their cup of tea, she being more enthusiastic about having a chat than her fellow editor who was keen to have an early afternoon finish and pick up his two children from school. They briefed him on the week they had had, mentioned a couple of minor things they thought he should know about and in return asked a few questions about the Thompson Newspaper Group. It was all very friendly, if a bit stilted at times. Only Ellen invited him over to see her team, which Dick thought was telling.

In London Richard Orange's letter on behalf of the Broad Bottom Herald Express landed on Deputy Chief Constable

Ryan Johnston's solicitor's desk at 4.30pm, but the recipient was out and not due back that day. It lay unopened.

*

After Ellen McCraken and Adrian Wall left, the latter in too much of a hurry for his own good, Dick called in on Lulu Popplewell to check everything was well in her department. He intended to head back to the Royal Imperial, change out of his suit and go for a decent walk along one of the nearby beaches before enjoying a hearty dinner. He had missed the sandwich van at lunch-time.

Lulu was her usual cheerful self, but took him on one side.

"I know my team got off to a bad start with you because of their breakfast antics, but they are a good bunch in the main. I wonder if it will be alright tomorrow morning if we do what we normally do when we hit our targets and have a bit of a celebration with cake and coffee which can be quite noisy for around 15 minutes?"

He smiled. He had no objection to a bit of light relief at the back end of the week once the papers were put to bed.

"Do you have a bran tub?" he enquired.

She gave him a quizzical look. "Why do I need one of those?"

"Place it in the room near your office, fill it with sawdust and bury different bars of chocolate bought out of petty cash. When anyone does particularly well either on a single day or over a week stop what everyone is doing and invite the rep to dig for her chocolate. Every now and then fill the tub with other treats."

Lulu thought it was a lovely idea which would go down well with her staff.

"Want to join us tomorrow at ten o'clock?"

"I just might," he replied and with that he went back, carefully locked the sideboard and the boardroom, which he had discovered only yesterday had unbreakable windows and the strongest doors in the building. He was happy to leave a copy of Mrs Johnston's file in the middle of a pile of old newspapers at the bottom of the sideboard.

He had just enough time the following morning to enjoy the advertising department's celebrations before heading for St Mawgan airport where he caught the noon flight to Stansted. He was surprised the driver of the Essex 'taxi' sent to pick him up was Jack Wilde, but it made sense because they were able to chat freely without interruption all the way to Torchester.

Jack was keen to discuss more than the Herald Express's looming libel action.

"What do you make of the set-up down there?

"Do you think some of the people have potential?

"What sort of managing director does it need?

"When can I expect a written report?"

The questions came thick and fast. Dick tackled the last question first.

"As long as I can get on with it and the lawyers don't need me for too long I intend to start writing something for you next week. However, I have a gut feeling there is more I need to know about some of the things I have discovered."

Dick told him about Rufus Jones and the two reporters with their ridiculous ties. He knew Jack would not be amused – he wasn't.

"If I didn't know it would make it difficult to produce a bi-weekly paper I would authorise you to get rid of the three of them right now. But that chap Tim Fletcher doesn't sound the sort of guy who could cope with too much pressure."

Dick gave him the good news. He thought Ellen McCraken had real potential and that Lulu Popplewell was a good advertising manager, respected by her team and had just the right décolletage.

"I promise I am not trying to ease you into the managing director's job, unless, of course you want it, but I would like you to see this particular job through," said Jack.

"I believe you will ferret out anything untoward and give the new man, whoever he might be, a good start. Whatever immediate on-the-spot action you take in the coming days or weeks I will back you 100 per cent."

They batted several matters back and forth between them before they reached Torchester. It gave Dick the chance to make it clear he did not want to live in Cornwall. He jokingly said Mary would divorce him after all he had told her so far.

Jack smiled. "I hear they get three types of weather in the far south west – it's either raining, has just rained, or is about to rain."

Now it was Dick's turn to smile. "You can do me one favour, Jack. Get someone to do a comparison with some of our other papers with regard to staff numbers, including the production department. A salary comparison would also be useful."

They went in separate directions when they arrived at head office, home of the Torchester Evening Gazette. Dick took the flight of steps to his office two at a time, much to Margaret his secretary's amusement.

117

She followed him at a more sedate pace. "The Cornish air must be doing you good," she said.

"The reason I bounced up those stairs for the first time for many years is that I am so delighted to be back in the land of the living," he told her.

"Oh, and there is me thinking it was because you could not wait to see me."

He looked at his desk where four neat piles of papers and a stack of correspondence which she had either answered or which needed his attention awaited him.

There was no news from Richard Orange that afternoon or the next day. Dick demolished the pile of correspondence, read a couple of the group's weekly papers, dictated memos about stories he felt had not been developed or were badly written and departed for home soon after 3pm on Friday afternoon. He aimed to spend the rest of the day and the weekend just with his wife. He felt he had earned it.

CHAPTER TWELVE

When Archibald Lang of respected London solicitors Hart and Lang flipped through his post soon after nine o'clock on Friday morning, which his secretary had opened for him, it didn't take him long to spot the letter from Richard Orange. They were hardly intimate friends – nobody in the legal profession had been elevated to that position – but they knew each other and had chatted a few times at several social events duty had forced both of them to attend.

When the holding letter had arrived earlier in the week Archibald had suspected the Deputy Chief Constable's wish to have the matter settled quickly with a published apology, agreed damages and payment of his legal bill was wishful thinking unless the newspaper really had no evidence to back up their claims about his client's extra-marital affairs.

It was possible that if all went well it would probably cost the Herald Express in the region of £20,000 plus their own legal bill if they gave up the fight this week. If legal horns were locked, the bill could run into six figures.

He had already warned Ryan Johnston that libel was a rich man's game and that many people who tried to get satisfaction in the courts ended up wishing they had never started.

The Johnston family had used Hart and Lang for their wildly varied legal arrangements and dealings for nearly 40 years. Old man Johnston, Ryan's father, was the closest friend Archibald would own up to and his death had reduced him to tears – in private, of course. In truth, he didn't care much for the son, but he had done well enough for himself and risen through different police forces to his present position. Word was, however, that he should not expect to go much further. He was regarded as a safe pair of hands rather than anything more dynamic.

Archibald knew he had to read between the lines when it came to letters he received from fellow solicitors on behalf of their clients. They have their own coded language. He studied what Richard Orange had written for ten minutes and the tingle down his back, which had served him well over the years, told him this was not going to be an easy battle to win. He was not an impulsive man, but if he had been he would have telephoned Mr Johnston there and then to say there was a conflict of interest and they could not represent him any further. He might even have suggested another firm who would handle the case. But he didn't.

Instead he reached for the internal phone and asked his secretary to find his client – he had proved rather elusive some days – and tell him he felt they ought to have an immediate meeting, even though he knew that getting into central London on a Friday would not be easy for the Deputy Chief Constable.

"Tell him it would be unfortunate if his duties detained him in Essex all day," he instructed her. "I need his agreement as to how we should proceed."

Ryan Johnston was in his office listening to reports on a drink-driving campaign they had run across two counties when his secretary interrupted to say he had an urgent call. He was in a reasonably good mood because the campaign had caught 214 drivers over the limit and sent a clear message that the police were leading the fight to cut road accident deaths on his patch at least.

Anyway, that was what the press release sent out in his name to all the newspapers in East Anglia said. All of them had a picture of him in their files if they wished to use it. He hoped they would.

His mood quickly changed when he picked up the phone and Archibald Lang's secretary was put through to him. When she said Mr Lang urgently needed to see him in London he knew it had to be bad news. He put her on hold while he asked his colleagues to take a tea break and leave him alone while he took an important call. When they had gone he insisted on speaking to his solicitor right away because if he could help it he didn't want to alter his Friday timetable.

When Archibald Lang read him Richard Orange's letter Ryan changed his mind during the short and very much to the point telephone call. They agreed it would be wise not to say too much over the phone. Ryan returned to his meeting, but now had lost all interest in the drink-driving figures.

"I hope it was not bad news," said a chief superintendent on his return.

"Actually it is. I need to go to London to deal with a family matter. Can you manage without me? I can read the minutes next week. Keep up the good work."

He picked up his briefcase, told his secretary the same story and was out of the building within five minutes of taking Archibald Lang's telephone call. I haven't lied, he mused. It is a family matter.

He knew it was totally against police procedure not to leave a telephone number where he could be contacted in the next few hours, but he felt it was a risk worth taking. He went home, changed out of his uniform and drove to Torchester railway station. A fast London train came in five minutes later. He stared out of the window all the way into Liverpool Street station from where a taxi got him to Hart and Lang's doorstep exactly 90 minutes after the solicitor's phone call.

There were no preliminaries. Archibald Lang handed him the letter to read for himself and sat back to watch Ryan's reaction. It wasn't long coming.

"Just what have they got on me and, more importantly, who did they get it from?"

It was a worrying start to their meeting, thought the solicitor, virtually an admission there was something he had not been told. Instinct told him his client had not been totally honest with him when he had come to him for advice about taking legal action against the Broad Bottom Herald Express

"I have no idea and won't have until you decide to issue a writ. At some stage in the coming months the Herald Express's legal team will have to reveal their defence, but we are several steps away from that at the moment. Libel actions can be long drawn out affairs."

The Deputy Chief Constable was aghast at the thought of this dragging out over many months. It was the last thing he wanted. He had enough on his plate with his job and the work he needed to put in to make future House of Commons lunches successful. His final payment depended on a successful outcome.

Archibald Lang jolted him further. "I think it is my duty to remind you that before you decide what to do next you should consider the financial implications. I will have to engage a barrister on your behalf and they don't come cheap. If you lose you will have a large bill to pay."

Ryan Johnston needed time to think. Marie-Clementine was not coming to stay the weekend. He had no idea where she was going to be over the next few days. When he had quizzed her about her movements two nights ago she had hinted she was dealing with a 'family matter', which left him just as ill informed as she wanted him to be.

It was a pity, he thought, *because she would know what to do*. He badly needed an ally.

"I will get back to you early next week," he told Archibald Lang. "We don't have to rush our reply, do we?"

The solicitor agreed they should not act hastily, but felt the need to inform his client it was in his own best interests to be totally honest with him.

"Have you any idea what information the newspaper might have got hold of which will make it difficult for you to succeed in your action?" he asked. "Is there something in your private life I should know about?"

Ryan Johnston sounded calmer than he felt.

"No, nothing. Absolutely nothing." And with that he left without shaking hands.

He might be his father's son, but he doesn't have his father's good manners, thought the elderly solicitor, who did not like the growing feeling he had that they might not win this case. He knew it would not be good for his company's reputation if they didn't.

✳

The Deputy Chief Constable's journey back to Torchester was just as quick as his trip into London. He managed to avoid the chaos of the early Friday rush hour and, thankfully, did not meet anybody he knew. He was so engrossed in his own thoughts he was surprised when the train stopped and he realised it had reached his destination.

Back in police headquarters he asked his secretary if anyone had called. She had not approved of his dashing off without telling her where he was going.

"There are a couple of messages on your desk and some post. I think somebody popped their head round the door while I was making coffee; it could have been the Chief Constable."

It was a lie, but he didn't know that. She knew that would worry him. That made her happy.

It seemed he had not really been missed by anyone important. There were few callers that Friday afternoon, which gave him time to do even more thinking. He had to know what information the Herald Express held on him and who had supplied it. Without the former he would not know the answer to the latter. He knew it would eat away at him until he got answers.

He was reasonably sure nobody in Torchester knew about Marie-Clementine, or the other two women he had had a liaison with several years ago. Both had gone to live abroad. As far as he knew they had not told any third party about their affairs, but he could not be certain. He knew the uncertainty would eat away at him.

He was less certain as to whether after a few drinks he had been indiscreet with some of his male friends, but there was absolutely nothing in any of his drawers or filing cabinets to link him with another woman – not even a birthday card.

. He was also fairly certain that even if he was questioned about the lunches he was co-hosting at the House of Commons he could claim he was simply helping a friend forge good international relationships. Any suggestion that he and Miss Dubois were engaged in anything more than a business relationship would be denied and possibly lead to legal action. He believed his position gave him some clout and authority.

But what could he do to ensure he won an apology from the Herald Express and a decent pay-off? As far as he could tell three people held information which might or might not ruin his career: a London solicitor, the Herald's editor in Cornwall and the person who had given them something which could ruin him. Suddenly he knew what he had to do. It was time to call in a few favours.

CHAPTER THIRTEEN

When Dick's taxi from St Mawgan airport dropped him at the office on Monday morning he was surprised to find a police car outside and what by Cornish standards constituted some sort of bustle. Even more surprising was the fact Tim Fletcher and Tony Morrisey had beaten him into work.

"There's a first for everything," he muttered to the startled driver, but in reality to nobody in particular.

He paid for the taxi, grabbed both his suitcase and briefcase and went to see what all the fuss was about. The front door was open, but nobody was in reception. It was only when he went through to the editorial department that Tim greeted him.

"We have been burgled," he blurted out. "And to make matters worse my secretary is on holiday this week."

Why the two were related was something Dick could not fathom; *it must be something in the local air*, he thought.

The news room was certainly a mess, but then again it never looked orderly. Organised chaos was how his first editor had described the state of things in most editorial departments. The floor was covered with files, reports, books, memos and a variety of other items many of which looked as though they had been scattered after being ejected from Edna Sparrow's now badly damaged filing cabinet.

"They have wrecked my office too," wailed Tim, which was something of an exaggeration.

Even so his filing cabinet had been forced with what Dick guessed was a crowbar.

"What I find unusual is that whoever it was doesn't appear to have taken anything," added the editor.

When Dick looked at the state of some of the typewriters, he wasn't surprised.

"And why did they only target me and my team?"

"They probably wanted an early look at all those fantastic stories you produce," explained Dick in an attempt to introduce some sarcastic humour into the proceedings.

He need not have bothered because Tim and Tony just gave him blank looks.

The two policemen, having had a look round, made a few notes and generally done very little, said their goodbyes. They would log the incident but as far as they were concerned nothing had been taken so they saw no need for it to take up too much of their time. To them it looked like a clear case of petty vandalism.

Dick didn't say anything. He had his own theory which he had no intention of sharing with Tim and Tony. He told them he would be back shortly – he needed to check the boardroom. He was relieved when he discovered it was still securely locked and there was no sign anyone had tried to enter. What puzzled him though was how anyone could have deactivated the office alarm system? They must have known the code. Whatever they were after, and by the minute he felt he knew what it was, they had not found it.

Tim and Tony were still full of doom and gloom when he returned to the news room. Dick thought the time for idle chat was over – action was required. At that moment Frank Helliwell came in. Before the production manager could join in any discussion about what and happened and who might be responsible, Dick took him on one side.

"I want you to let me have two of your men to help clear this up because we have a paper to get out tomorrow. If we leave it to the reporters they will have an excuse not to produce anything until late morning. I won't have that."

Frank understood. He didn't want to be home late either, given that he hoped to get in a round of golf that evening.

Five minutes later Jonny Grayson, a member of the press crew, and Bernard Webber, who Dick was told was a part-time 'reader' checking the advertisements and news pages for mistakes, started the job of returning some semblance of order to the news room.

Dick and Tim agreed that when Edna Sparrow returned from holiday she would have the job of filing things in their correct place. Until then they would be kept in a host of cardboard boxes.

Tim was left to make his own arrangements with regard to his filing cabinet after everyone had helped him with some initial cleaning up.

"I don't see any point in your team spending more than five minutes discussing the break-in," Dick told him. "It is your job to ensure it is as normal a Monday morning as possible."

The cleaning up operation did not take as long as had been expected. Nobody noticed Jonny slip several sheets of paper into his overalls and mark one of the boxes with a felt tip pen. He was sure Frank and the rest of the gang would be very interested in what he had discovered. Very interested indeed!

It was mid afternoon before Edna Sparrow heard about the burglary and it ruined her holiday. She lived alone in a two bedroomed bungalow near the top of a cliff with wonderful views out to sea. She was a spinster who had despised most men ever since she was jilted a month before her anticipated wedding day 20 years ago. Both her parents were dead. They had left her enough to pay off the mortgage on the bungalow and live comfortably. She had no family. She took two holidays a year – one in the sun somewhere in the Mediterranean and one staying with a fellow spinster in Hampshire where she was when she received news of the break-in.

The only consolation she could think of when she heard what had happened was that she was not abroad.

She told her friend about the burglary and made it out to be a far more serious incident than it was.

"They want me back as soon as possible," she lied. "Can I come again later in the year?"

An hour later she was in her car and heading for Broad Bottom. She prayed she was not too late.

Ryan Johnston was in his office when his secretary put through the call from two officers currently working for the Cornwall force.

"We had no difficulty getting into that office because the Herald Express's former owner gave us the code for the alarm several years ago. He used to go in at all hours and set the alarm without checking he had closed all the necessary doors. We got called out so many times when it belted out at odd hours that in the end he thought it was best if we had a key and knew the code"

So far so good, thought Ryan.

"We did as you said and targeted the news room and the editor's office. There was lots of material in one filing cabinet, including invoices and records of some scheme which looked distinctly like it had very little to do with producing newspapers. There was nothing remotely like the stuff you asked us to look for."

Ryan swore.

"And before you ask we were thorough. We spent four hours going through everything. We thought we had hit the jackpot when in the editor's filing cabinet we discovered a folder containing a couple of legal actions, but they were old and nothing to do with you."

There was silence for a few moments. For once Ryan was lost for words. Eventually he rallied.

"I am sure you did your best. I am grateful, really I am – just disappointed."

He put the phone down.

He was far more than disappointed. He sensed he was losing control. What was it Archibald Lang had told him about many people coming to regret it when they took legal action? Two weeks ago he had been in charge; now he wasn't sure what to do.

He still had no idea that the people he was dealing with were on his doorstep and not based in Cornwall. If he had known that the man currently in charge of the Broad Bottom Herald Express was the Thompson Group's editorial director Dick Chinnery he would have thought long and hard about his next steps. But he didn't.

At that moment his secretary told him the Chief Constable wanted to see him.

In London Marie-Clementine Dubois was having a better day. She met two of her Russian contacts at a coffee house in Islington. They were well pleased with the information they had gleaned and the people their representatives had met at the House of Commons lunches she had organised. She handed over the proposed guest list for the next one in four weeks' time. They scanned it, noting the names and titles of several government ministers in the midst of other lesser establishment figures used as cover. They were men of few words, but many expressions. They gave her the go-ahead.

She was less pleased when back at her flat she took a telephone call from one of the Russians who told her she was being followed. She had no idea until then that somebody might be monitoring her movements. Exactly who that someone might be was something of a mystery. It was time for Ryan to be useful – he could earn his keep for once.

She instinctively looked out of her window and could not see anyone obviously hanging around. Her flat was in a very security conscious block, so she had no fears there. All the same it was disconcerting that she would now have to be on her guard.

Several other people were also not happy. They met to share their sandwiches and various cakes at the far end of the Herald Express press room where Jonny Grayson produced a sheaf of papers which until last night had been safely tucked away in Edna Sparrow's filing cabinet.

"No wonder we didn't get the money we asked for at the end of last year," said Frank Helliwell, who had joined them after checking Tuesday's Herald Express was on course to be finished on time.

"I just knew something wasn't right. I nearly got it out of her when we met for a drink at the Red Lion last Tuesday."

The thought of Frank getting anything out of Edna was met with incredulity by the rest of them.

Once they had all had their say they agreed somebody would have to have strong words with Edna, but initially none of them had a clue how to go about it without threatening what up to now was a very lucrative sideline.

Frank said he thought they should first approach the chairman of the estate agents' consortium and without raising too many hackles find out how long the editorial secretary had been receiving her private retainer on top of an eighth share of their combined earnings. When they agreed with him and he got the task, he wished he had kept his mouth shut.

When Dick was convinced that normal service had been resumed in the office he made himself a cup of coffee in the boardroom and rang Jack Wilde in Torchester to tell him what had happened and also discuss his suspicions.

"This was no ordinary burglary. The only thing that was taken was a mars bar from a reporter's desk. They didn't make any mess in the advertising or production departments and as far as I can tell did not try and force their way into the boardroom. I have a gut feel it has everything to do with the Johnston legal action and the documents we hold. How the alarm was deactivated is a mystery."

Jack listened intently. Until now he had left everything with Dick, but he felt the time was ripe for him to offer some help. He hadn't lived in Essex all his life without making many useful contacts - one of them was the current Chief Constable, Keith Wood. As soon as Dick put the phone down he called in his secretary and re-arranged his diary.

He had never used the 'hot line' number the Chief Constable had given him several years ago at a police media briefing 'to call if the occasion ever arose'. He felt it was an appropriate time to make use of it. Mr Wood's secretary kept him waiting a few minutes but when she returned she told him that if he was able to visit county police headquarters the Chief Constable would be happy to have a chat with him in half an hour.

The two men had known each other since school and although their careers had taken different paths, they shared a number of common interests. While most people had only seen the sterner side of the Chief Constable's character, Jack knew that he loved his growing family, played a decent game of bridge, supported his local rugby club and had a sharp sense about what was morally right and wrong.

It helped Jack's case now that on several occasions he had helped the police with their enquiries and twice had suppressed stories for a couple of days on police advice so both a rapist and potential terrorist could be apprehended.

They did not waste time on general chat. The Chief Constable was surprised to learn that the Thompson Newspaper Group had other business interests at the far end of the country. Henry Thompson had not told him that when they had last met, but why should he? It took him a split second to realise the next few minutes might be about his deputy.

Jack didn't go into too much detail about the Herald Express stories. Instead he explained why Dick Chinnery was spending most of his week in Cornwall, a general outline of the documents he had been given by a very angry Mrs Johnston, after her husband had sent a threatening legal letter, and his and Dick's suspicions about the burglary.

Keith Wood knew his deputy's wife; in his opinion she was not a woman to be messed around with. She had been a strong force behind her husband's rise through the ranks and on the couple of occasions she had cooked a meal for him and his wife it had been delicious; both had enjoyed her company. She had done a good job of bringing up the two Johnston children 'the right way' while her husband was furthering his police career.

He told Jack he would never have thought of her as the sort of woman who would run off with another woman, "but then who knows anyone really?"

"I think we might be able to help each other," he said. "I presume you were planning to give me the documents at some stage in case they involve something my force would be interested in?"

Jack smiled.

"Indeed I was when our lawyers have had the chance to analyse them. I think they strengthen our case considerably, but I still have some worries that we will end up with a big legal bill. I am not sure a jury will be sympathetic to a wife who leaves her husband for another woman. They might regard her as the classical woman scorned seeking revenge."

The Chief Constable wasn't a man given to instant decisions, but on this occasion he felt he needed to move quickly to limit any potential damage to his force's image.

"I would like to handle this in an unofficial way. You let me have a copy of those documents today, which I promise I will not use to compromise any defence you mount against Deputy Chief Constable Johnston, and I will make some enquiries internally that would be impossible for you to make on your own. Is it a deal?"

Jack smiled again. He was not used to it – he thought his face might crack if he continued smiling. A deal it was – and a good one at that. They shook hands on it. The meeting was over. Both men didn't believe in wasting words or time.

When Jack left the Chief Constable remained at his desk and made some notes. Then he rang an internal number and asked to see the last three months' call log for Deputy Chief Constable Ryan Johnston's telephone. He got it within the hour and it made very interesting reading. It was the recent calls to and from Cornwall which intrigued him the most.

His secretary brought in an envelope marked personal while he was scanning the call list. It did not take him long to realise the contents would have to be passed on to a higher authority as soon as he had kept his promise to Jack Wilde. He rang his opposite number in the westcountry and in no time at all he had the names of the two detectives he now believed had broken into the Herald Express office.

It was early evening when he and Jack had their second meeting of the day, this time at the Chief Constable's request. But at this one two other people were present – Arthur Nightingale from the Met and 'Larry' representing MI5 - no surname was offered or asked for. Both had seen the documents Jack had sent the Chief Constable.

It was the man from the Met who took the lead.

"Mr Wood has assured us you can be totally trusted."

He looked at Jack.

"He has also vouched for your editorial director who we already know a bit about after his run-in with Thurnham Council and its masonic lodge six years ago. However, we would prefer it if everything I am going to tell you is strictly limited to the pair of you and your solicitor."

Jack nodded his agreement.

"It means you will have to sign the Official Secrets Act within the next 24 hours."

Jack wondered where all this was going. Over the next fifteen minutes he found out.

"What we would like you to do is play for time so we can continue unhindered with our undercover operation," said Arthur Nightingale.

"What you have given us is invaluable. It means we can confidently close down a nasty little operation much quicker than we had originally thought."

Jack had no hesitation in assuring him the Thompson Newspaper Group would play its part.

" I can assure you right now there is no chance of Mr Johnston winning his libel action because, if necessary, we will provide you with enough evidence to plead the defence of truth", added Arthur.

"Somehow, I don't think the case will progress very far, but first of all we want to find out exactly who is funding Miss Dubois and who has already been compromised. The Home Secretary is taking a keen interest in this and I understand is reporting direct to the Prime Minister."

Wow, thought Jack. Even he with all his experience had never handled a case like this.

"What about the two detectives in Cornwall?"

"They are small fry," said the Chief Constable. "Rest assured their careers in the police force will come to an abrupt end very soon, but only when the time is right."

Larry said very little. He just watched Jack. When he was happy with the managing director and his responses he signalled it was time the meeting was over.

*

A telephone call and thirty minutes later Dick was packing a toiletries bag, a book and a few other personal items and was on his way to Penzance where he caught Monday night's overnight sleeper train to London Paddington and from there a fast train to Torchester. He was met by his managing director who took him to his home, sat him down and for the next hour told him all that had been agreed in the Chief Constable's office the night before.

Dick had taken the precaution of removing the all-important documents from their hiding place in the Herald Express boardroom sideboard just in case there was an unlikely second attempt to find them. Jack Wilde burnt them. There was no need to keep them now they were in the hands of their solicitor, the Chief Constable and MI5. For all he knew Mrs Thatcher had a copy.

Later that Tuesday morning the pair of them duly signed the Official Secrets Act at Torchester police headquarters after which they travelled the short distance to their offices.

Margaret Evans was extremely surprised to see Dick when he popped his head round her door for a brief catch-up.

"Are you Batman now?" she enquired.

"Superman," he retorted, although he didn't feel all that super; he hadn't slept very well on the train and had not enjoyed the rush hour Tube ride. He had marvelled how people did it five days a week.

He had the same surprise effect later when after dealing with some paperwork a taxi took him to the Thurnham and Shaldon Standard's office where his wife was approaching deadline. She held him close for several minutes and started to fire lots of questions at him, but suddenly stopped when she realised she still had a paper to produce.

"Save it," he said as he pressed a finger against her lips. "I have booked a table for us at the Chequers Inn this evening. However, I don't want to be out too late because I have to catch that early morning flight again from Stansted to St Mawgan." Margaret had already booked him a seat.

Mary knew her husband well enough not to press him further and anyway she was needed in her news room. He went home to grab a shower and a change of clothing.

Over dinner he brought her up to date about the burglary and his suspicions it was connected with Deputy Chief

Constable Johnston. She already knew about the documents, but not their contents. When she asked why he had come back on the overnight train for an urgent meeting with Jack, he did not tell any lies, but he skirted round some of the facts. He felt there was no harm in letting her know that his boss had used his connections to discover who the burglars were, but the involvement of the security services was something it was best she did not know about at this stage. Anyway, he didn't want her to be overly concerned. After what happened six years ago with Toby Walters and his thugs he knew she would definitely worry if she knew the full story. There would be a proper time place to fill in the details. Hopefully, he thought, it would be sooner rather than later.

Mary had the good sense not to probe any further. Instead, she told him about the stories which would be appearing in that week's Standard. She made him laugh. He loved her sense of humour – it was one of the first things that had attracted him when she was a reporter and he was her editor. Together they had produced the Standard for eight weeks during the 1979 journalists' strike when due to an oversight by a branch official she was the only reporter not a member of any union.

She held his hands across the table. For her nights like this were precious. She knew he needed her support and for her to be by his side. It was a role she was more than happy to play. She also sensed he wasn't telling her the full story.

"Before I forget I must tell you about one highly amusing incident today," she whispered so nobody else could have any chance of hearing.

"I don't think you know Barry Guest. He has only been with us a few months but in that time we have noticed how he doffs his cap at anybody remotely in authority. He is in his late forties and will be a useful addition to the team, but the younger reporters have already started gently ribbing him."

Dick knew she would not stand anything which smacked of office bullying, but humour was a vital ingredient of a good news room. He let her continue.

"He did a story about Lord Errol James who lives in that historical house out in the country the other side of Tillingham, and got some dates wrong. They were relatively minor, yet annoying mistakes. Most people would not have complained. His Lordship couldn't get hold of me so left a message to say he would ring back."

Dick laughed. He had seen how tactful Mary was in handling frivolous complaints – one ear to the phone while she corrected a reporter's copy with her free hand.

"When Barry came back into the office he was all of jitter when the others told him who was 'after his blood'. One of them, who is a very good mimic, went into another office, dialled Barry's number and pretended to be Lord James. It was hilarious."

"Didn't he cotton on as to what was happening?" enquired Dick.

"Not until the end when the rogue Lord James said you are a silly arse Mr Guest. What are you?"

When Barry muttered down the phone 'I am a silly arse your lordship' the entire news room exploded in laughter and he knew he had been had. He took it very well."

Half an hour later Dick was tucked up in his own bed. Mary set the alarm for 5am and jumped in next to him. He was fast asleep, but had a smile on his face. She cuddled up next to him.

CHAPTER FOURTEEN

It was the private detective's bad luck that Marie-Clementine Dubois was not planning to see her boyfriend for several days. He had followed her to her coffee meeting and watched as she had laughed her way through what looked like no more than friends enjoying each other's company. He made a note that her two male companions looked more like Russians or Latvians than senior Essex policemen. He had a picture of Ryan Johnston and he definitely wasn't present. Both these man were much younger and looked far fitter.

When she returned to her flat after doing some shopping the detective slipped round the corner and took the opportunity to phone his contact at Private Eye. They compared notes. He stood watch for several hours, but she showed no sign of going out and as far as he could see she did not have any visitors looking like her boyfriend. He called it a day at ten o'clock and headed home to write up the report he knew Jack Wilde would want. He failed to spot somebody was watching him.

Ryan Johnston was kept far too busy on a visit to the Suffolk coast and a boring meeting of Neighbourhood Watch co-ordinators on Monday to think about another quick trip into London. He spoke to Archibald Lang on the phone and between them they agreed to wait for a further response from Richard Orange to their claim for damages.

"It is normal to put some pressure on and insist on a reply within seven days, but I think it would be wise to give them at least 14 days to respond, or even longer. There no real rush. It pays to be patient and see what your opponent has in his hand."

The solicitor liked to use bridge metaphors.

Ryan's meeting with the Chief Constable last Friday had been routine – thank goodness. There was no mention of his wife or the newspaper stories concerning her new relationship. It was a sign of how worried he was that a simple call to attend a standard end-of-the-week meeting had given him the jitters. He knew he had to get a grip. Marie-Clementine had told him off and warned him he should show a bit more steel when he had called her over the weekend. She had not done that before. All of a sudden he felt alone and vulnerable. The small house he rented was cold and empty and he now had to make his own dinner most evenings. He slept badly for the fourth consecutive night.

*

Dick's surprise return to Torchester less than 24 hours after arriving on Monday morning had tongues wagging at the Broad Bottom Herald Express throughout Tuesday. Speculation was rife, but most people concluded he had gone back to head office to report on the burglary and receive some instructions. His early Wednesday morning flight from Stansted was delayed by 90 minutes because of fog so by the time he got to the Herald's office nearly everybody was already at work. The gossips among them were even more baffled by his swift return.

He did not like the smell of fried food which immediately assailed his nostrils; *it stinks like a transport cafe*, he thought. When Lulu Popplewell came into the boardroom he politely but firmly asked her to do something about it. She agreed the smell was particularly obnoxious this morning. He guessed the breakfast club had thought he wouldn't be back so soon.

The only surprise was when he saw Edna Sparrow walking across the car park carrying a large box. His curiosity peeked, he couldn't resist greeting her in the reception area.

"Aren't you supposed to be on holiday?"

She didn't know whether he was being extremely inquisitive or genuinely caring about her holidays.

"I thought Tim and Tony would need me when I heard about the burglary. I came in yesterday and helped put some things back in their rightful place and then took several boxes home with me to sort out. It will take some time to get everything back in its right order."

For some reason he couldn't fathom he didn't believe her.

"That is extremely thoughtful of you but actually I press-ganged a couple of guys into service and they did a fairly good job."

If she recognised the pun, she didn't show it.

Edna could have done without this conversation. She was not in the best of tempers, but she was shrewd enough not to overstep the mark with an editorial director who seemed to have been given power of near life and death over the office. It was a good job, she thought, that he didn't know the real reason why she had had no option but to dash back from Hampshire. For a fleeting moment she thought he did, then dismissed it as paranoia.

Whoever had gone through her filing cabinet had flung the entire contents all over the place and potentially had already done untold damage. It seemed she was the main victim of Sunday night's break-in.

"Do you need any help with that box or anything else you have brought from home?" asked Dick.

She shook her head but she allowed him to go ahead and open doors through which she disappeared into the editorial department, where just about everybody was too busy bashing their typewriters to even acknowledge her presence.

Rufus Jones caught her eye, but did not say anything. He was still smarting about his written warning and thought that if anyone had shopped him it would have been Edna. He couldn't believe for one minute that any readers had taken the trouble to complain simply because they had managed to sell their unwanted items a day or two early. Yes, it must be Edna. He had seen the smirk on her face when she had taken notes at his disciplinary hearing. He would get his own back one day.

She ignored him; he reinforced her opinion of men. She summed them up in one word – trouble.

Last night she had received a distressing call from Frank Helliwell who had told her he wanted an urgent chat *'on behalf of the rest of their team'*. It had not taken her long to discover that when the contents of her filing cabinet had been strewn across the news room floor her secret back-hander from the estate agents had been revealed. There was no way she was going to meet him at the Red Lion again after the fuss she had made the other evening, and it could not be during normal hours when too many ears were finely tuned. Also, she needed time to prepare her defence. However, for once Frank had been insistent - it had to be that week.

"Ok, the office is usually empty on Thursday nights apart from the part-time van drivers collecting different papers and the press crew finishing off printing the Herald Express. Why don't we meet in the kitchen at eight o'clock?"

He agreed – she had bought some time to try and find out exactly which papers were missing.

If there was one person Dick was pleased to see that Wednesday it was Ellen McCraken. She came alone. She explained that fellow editor Adrian had a pile of pages to proof read and would call in later. He offered her a cup of tea which she gladly accepted.

"Do you mind if I take off my shoes? They are new and are killing me," she asked him.

He told her to kick them anywhere she wanted. He was used to his wife doing the same.

"Provide me with some sane conversation about the stories you are featuring this week plus anything about your future plans," he told her. "So far this week I have done everything but get involved with the work I enjoy the most – running a newspaper."

She knew as much as anyone else in the office about the burglary and was equally baffled about its purpose. She decided to let him broach the subject if he wanted to, otherwise she would leave it well alone. It really was nothing to do with her – the elderly citizens of Crackington by Sea were 'outraged' if there was more than one serious burglary a year in their gentile town.

It stimulated her to be able to chat with someone who understood how a news room operated and what made a good story. Harvey Fairbanks certainly didn't and she did not rate Tim Fletcher who had not offered any support when was it was needed last year. She often thought the Herald Express could be so much better in the right hands: its half developed stories were rarely followed up the next week; it lacked a campaigning edge when the right local issues arose; and regularly failed to touch any story which might upset the establishment. They added up to a shocking indictment of Tim's editorship, she believed.

"I like the number of letters you print each week," Dick commented as together they leafed through the previous week's paper. "Thank goodness you don't allow letter writers to be anonymous."

It was one of his pet hates. They were banned on all his Essex and Suffolk papers unless people could give a good reason why they should have anonymity.

"If people want to air their strong opinions they should have the courage of their convictions to put their name to what they have written," he told her.

Ellen could not agree more, but thought he would have a fit if he ever found the time to analyse past editions of the Herald Express. She hoped he would be around long enough to make the necessary improvements she knew were needed. She, for one, had been delighted when Harvey Fairbanks had sold the company. The longer she chatted with Dick the more she believed he would bring about major changes as long as he did not have to keep doing 700 mile round trips twice a week. Tim Fletcher had better watch out.

Ellen revelled in telling him about the towns and villages her two papers covered and some of the stories in that week's papers. He, in turn, was impressed with the way she praised various members of her small editorial team and talked about 'us' and 'we'.

"We have a good story on the front page this week about plans to build 18 giant wind turbines on hills outside the village of Walton. They will be 80 metres high – taller than Nelson's column and half the height of Blackpool Tower. The three rotor blades on each turbine will be 66 metres across. The aim is to provide enough electricity for 22,000 homes in Cornwall."

It is the sort of story that will run and run, thought Dick, but he did not interrupt her while she was now in full flow. Her enthusiasm for her work did her much credit in his eyes.

"I am chairing a public meeting on Saturday afternoon because as you can imagine the locals are not too happy about such a large number of turbines desecrating one of the area's major sites of natural beauty, popular with walkers and wildlife enthusiasts alike."

She happily chatted about other stories until his phone rang. It was Margaret Evans to tell him she had re-booked his flight home for Friday morning rather than tomorrow afternoon. He didn't know it then but he wouldn't make that flight.

It was Ellen's cue to leave. She looked at her watch and realised she needed to get back to the production area. She walked out of the boardroom with a spring in her step.

Dick made a mental note to compare what she produced with her small team of journalists to what was done by the other two editors with their larger staffs over a longer period than a single week. He thought he already knew what the results would be, but for the moment he would give both of them the benefit of the doubt.

He spent the rest of his working day fielding calls from his Essex and Suffolk editors who were approaching their own deadlines and needed varying pieces of advice, or simply wanted to get his opinion on a story.

Jack Wilde also phoned to say he had been in contact with their private detective and between them they had decided there was no point in continuing the surveillance of Miss Dubois. His report would be awaiting Dick when he was next in Torchester, but, given what he now knew, Jack said he was fairly relaxed. He had told Richard Orange to do whatever was necessary to stall the legal process. The lawyer had assured Jack it would not be difficult. He too had signed the Official Secrets Act.

CHAPTER FIFTEEN

Apart from his usual Thursday morning meeting with Lulu Popplewell, during which she updated him on the new policy with regard to accepting late advertising, Thursday was a day when Dick managed to get to grips with several outstanding issues, find time to have a 20 minute chat with his wife in her Thurnham office and also remember to look out for the sandwich man.

Lulu had done some research and discovered four local businesses in Broad Bottom and two in both Crackington and Piddle Wood had for many months consistently delayed booking their adverts until the last minute. They had managed to achieve a 45% reduction on what they should have paid and also got their advertisements onto prime early right hand pages - the pages readers went to first.

"What happened today then?" enquired Dick.

"We didn't call them – they called us. I arranged for every prime slot to be already taken and the few places available were right at the back of each paper. I was lucky this week because there was higher demand than usual," she said.

"Five of them panicked when we did not make our usual late call offering cheap advertising rates. I had asked for all such calls to come direct to me and was sweetness and light with them. If you want their names I can let you have them, but you will find their adverts on left hand pages well back in both the Herald Express and Times - they have been given only the usual ten per cent discount for regular customers."

"I bet they don't wait until Thursday morning next week," said Dick.

She chuckled.

"They haven't. All five have already booked a right hand page for the next four weeks. Word will soon get around; it is like that round here."

Dick knew his standing with the advertising reps had just rise a notch or two because their decent bonuses were based on sales revenue targets; if the company did well, so did they. He had no problem with that.

The light was fading when Edna Sparrow parked her car where it would not attract much attention. There was plenty of activity down one side of the Herald Express where vans were being loaded with papers which would go to wholesalers across

Cornwall. Other vans would do more direct deliveries to larger newsagents in the main towns. She entered the building by a side door. There was just enough light for her to make her way into the editorial department to collect a few items before her meeting with Frank Helliwell.

She had prepared the best arguments she could as to why she had been taking a bigger cut than the rest of them. It had been disappointing that she had still not been able to identify which documents had been taken. Hadn't the scheme been her idea in the first place? Didn't she have the job of meeting the estate agents on a regular basis to ensure they were happy? Surely the good relationships she had cultivated were worth something? In her heart she didn't think they would buy it, but what could they do about it? When last night she had realised there was not a lot they could do, she had slept soundly.

The more she thought about it, the more the burglary was a mystery. It didn't make any sense. Every reporter's desk and Tim Fletcher's drawers had been emptied while two filing cabinets, including her own, had been forced open. But why hadn't the advertising department been pulled apart or the production area? She reckoned it must have been to do with some story they had published. She would never know.

She had just turned the key in her new filing cabinet when she thought she heard a faint sound. She stopped what she was doing and listened for a clue as to where it came from.

All she could hear was the distant noise of vans being loaded with newspapers. She decided her mind was playing tricks. Then she heard it again.

It was one of the last sounds she would hear. A tie came round her neck, while a knee in her back forced her down on her knees. She tried to insert her fingers between the tie and her neck but 20 seconds later she was unconscious. Her wind-pipe was crushed which caused her arteries to stop supplying blood to her brain.

Frank Helliwell turned up for what he guessed would not be a pleasant meeting a few minutes after eight o'clock. He had been home for a meal and he returned just as the press did its final printing of the night. He exchanged brief hellos with a couple of staff, but was too pre-occupied with his imminent meeting with Edna to want to chat about sport, or anything else. He was surprised when he discovered she was not already in the kitchen – most unlike her to be late for any meeting. He did not know which entrance she would use, but he could see that none of the other office lights were on.

Thirty minutes later he decided she was not going to show.

"The cow," he muttered to nobody but himself. "She has ducked out at the last minute rather than face up to the truth about her deception."

And with that he went home.

*

Edna Sparrow's body was discovered by a part-time cleaner just before 6.30 on Friday morning. At first the cleaner thought someone had slept in the office after a heavy night's drinking; it had happened before. She dialled 999 and within 20 minutes what appeared to be the entire local police force were on the scene.

Detective Chief Inspector Bryan Lolly and Detective Sergeant Sebastian Walker arrived half an hour later at the same time as Dick Chinnery, who had forsaken breakfast when he got the news at his hotel.

The entire building was cordoned off, but after their initial inspection the two senior policemen agreed that was an over-reaction. Only the editorial department would be out of bounds for the foreseeable future.

Where were Tim Fletcher and Tony Morrisey when you needed them? thought Dick. He had his answer soon after when they arrived in the same car. Tim's car battery was flat.

"Only in Cornwall," uttered Dick well within their hearing range.

Neither editor nor chief reporter knew how to react to what had happened. Dick gave them the benefit of his doubts and put their dumb looks down to both the shock of the murder and the death of a colleague, even though she was unloved.

"I don't think you will get into the news room or your office for some time," Dick told them. "I am going to negotiate for typewriters and other items like notebooks and page plans to be removed by the police so we can do some work today. Perhaps the only fortunate thing is that it is a Friday. I suggest you get on the phone and arrange for a temporary secretary to come in to do the typing Edna would have done for you. She can also be responsible for making sure the police are offered plenty of refreshments."

With that he went to speak to DCI Lolly to see what concessions he could wring out of him.

When Dick returned he told editor and chief reporter a couple of constables had been given the task of carrying the equipment he had requested into the boardroom.

"I will move out. It is the only spare room you can feasibly use, but there are only two telephones."

Tim and Tony simply nodded their agreement.

Dick locked the sideboard, removed his tray of cups, the coffee pot and other items and left them in reception. He would sort out a new 'office' later.

As staff arrived in dribs and drabs they were ushered by Tony into the advertising department where they speculated wildly about what had happened. There were a few rumbling stomachs because there was no chance of a breakfast club gathering this morning.

While he waited for everyone to arrive at work, including the production team, Dick returned to the boardroom and rang Jack Wilde.

"Wow, even by your standards that is quite something," said the managing director. "What is it about you that attracts trouble in bucketfuls every now and then?"

Before Dick could answer Jack added: "What help do you need?"

He didn't think at this stage there was much that could be done from Torchester, but then changed his mind.

"Ring my wife, tell her what has happened and ask her to pack a suitcase with another pair of shoes for me. There are

164

plenty of trains to the south west from London on a Friday. Once I know which train she is on tell her I will pick her up at Bodmin Parkway. Her deputy editor is quite competent and can take over until she returns. It will be good to have my reporter wife by my side. She will love handling this story for the Broad Bottom Herald Express."

*

Jack agreed and within the hour Mary had a first class rail ticket and was on her way to Cornwall after remembering to cancel Sunday lunch with her mother and father.

"Have you got one of those free holiday breaks you told me travel companies give reporters if you write a kind article about your stay, even when it has been awful?" her father had asked.

"Dad, you know me better than that. Remember how I gave that holiday camp at Yarmouth a dreadful write-up last year?" But she did not answer his question.

*

Dick re-booked his room in Royal Imperial Hotel for the entire following week with the option of an extension. *Who knows how long this is going to take to sort out,* he thought. He then went to face the Herald's staff.

165

There was more a sense of shock than anything else when he told them Edna Sparrow had been murdered. He had initially thought it might be best to simply say it was an unexplained death, but after he had dwelt on it for a few minutes he realised that would fool nobody, even a collection of mainly dim-witted journalists. DCI Lolly had confirmed that murder was the only reasonable explanation. He tried hard not to spook them too much. There were relatively few questions and no tears. He promised to keep them informed, but he said Edna would have wanted them to carry on working. He didn't know if that was really true, but it seemed to fit what little he knew of her character.

Nobody had yet told Rufus Jones who rarely worked on a Friday.

Lulu Popplewell took Dick on one side after the meeting. "You are going to need an office because there are bound to be a lot of meetings. I am going to move out of mine and bunk up with the rest of my team. One of the reps is on holiday which means there is a spare desk. It won't do any harm for me to see them in action close up."

Up until then he had still not given much thought as to where he was going to work, but he realised she had a valid point. He didn't fancy trying to get any work done from the kitchen, so he thanked her and then went off to see what the two detectives wanted to happen next.

DS Walker told him Tim Fletcher's office would be used as their main room for conducting interviews and asked if he would he be kind enough to make himself available within the next ten minutes?

He headed back to the boardroom where the reporters and sub-editors appeared to be sorting themselves out. They stopped talking when he walked in, obviously not sure how they should react. He spotted Tony Morrissey and told him to appoint one reporter to start gathering together as much information as was currently available, but that an 'ace' reporter would be arriving late in the afternoon from Torchester to exclusively handle and write up all stories connected to the murder of Edna Sparrow.

He did not tell him it was his wife. That was something he and the rest of them would have to work out for themselves – if they ever did.

Dick took an instant liking to DCI Lolly when he became the first person to be formally interviewed. It was obvious from the opening questions that this was not some country copper out of his depth. Afterwards he wasn't sure how helpful he had been, but he went through the reasons why he was managing the show at the Herald Express and the circumstances surrounding the burglary. He had to tread carefully when talking about the latter. He realised he could not give any hint, even to a senior policeman, that there might be more to it than some opportunistic thieving.

DCI Lolly believed it was too co-incidental that the burglary had taken place only a few days before someone was murdered in the very same office, but he let it pass for the moment. Was it also just coincidence that the previous Friday his Chief Constable had shown him a couple of telephone numbers and asked him whose phones they belonged to at their Truro headquarters? When he had supplied the two names and asked why they were important he had been told the request had come from the Chief Constable of the East Anglian force based in Torchester.

Torchester! Wasn't that where this man Dick Chinnery said he was from? Two coincidences in one week? No way! There was something not quite right. He felt it in his water!

By the time Dick was satisfied the newspaper was returning to something like normal working and the editor and his reporters had everything they needed for the time being to get on with next Tuesday's paper, the two detectives had already started their first series of formal interviews with staff. Everyone who worked in the news room was asked what they knew about Edna Sparrow, her lifestyle, her friends and possibly enemies as they attempted to create a picture from which further questions would arise, along with possible clues as to the identity of her killer.

The obvious first question which needed answering was why anyone would want to kill a 48-year-old newspaper secretary who lived alone and had no close family? And why do it in her own office on a Thursday night when by all accounts she should not have been there? Why not at her relatively remote home? DCI Lolly quickly came to the conclusion that the answers had to be found inside the very building where he was sat.

He didn't expect the forensic boys to come up with much. Fingerprints were a waste of time. There were so many, all of them probably accountable for – he knew they would offer few clues. It was a pain-staking job, but it would have to be done all the same.

The tie which had been removed from around Edna Sparrow's neck was a different matter. He discovered it belonged to one of the Herald Express reporters. It had been bought in the Broad Bottom Oxfam shop the previous Saturday and according to its owner had been worn just once after he had been told on Monday morning to discard it – or else. He had bought another one to wear at work and left the offensive tie rolled up in the in-tray on his desk. His story was corroborated by three other reporters. Anyone could have taken it and strangled Edna Sparrow. DCI Lolly hoped it would reveal some clue, but again he had a feeling it wouldn't.

He turned to his colleague who had been diligently taking notes throughout each meeting.

"We need to speak to the Herald's editor a second time after what we have been told - just to clarify a few points. Ask him to come and join us."

Tim Fletcher was doing his best to rally his troops. A bit of reaction had set in and he could tell some of them were struggling to concentrate. He had reminded his chief reporter and sub editors they had to start work on Tuesday's paper – murder or no murder. He already knew what would be on the front page and on two pages inside unless someone was charged in the meantime. Even then it would not stop him doing a lengthy obituary on Edna. He had taken possession of a number of pictures showing police cars outside the front of the building and discovered a couple of pictures of her on file. She was even smiling on one of them!

"Nobody leaves tonight until we have done eight pages. We can do a weddings page and Down Memory Lane can take up half a page. The rest will need to be filled with stories I hope you already have in your notebooks. If not, start hitting the phones."

"But we only have two," observed one brave reporter. Tim glared at him.

At that moment DS Walker opened the door and asked if Tim could spare some more of his time. It was left to Tony to chivvy up the reporters.

There was not much else Tim could tell DCI Lolly he had not already gleaned from reading Edna's personnel record. She had worked at the Herald Express for 23 years and in addition to being a highly organised woman who ensured the smooth running of the office, she had produced a twice yearly listings and events magazine which attracted a sizeable amount of advertising.

The editor admitted she would be a difficult act to follow because she did many unseen and under-appreciated jobs. He believed they wouldn't really know everything she had done until they started to find out over the coming weeks. As an example of what he meant he said that only ten minutes ago he had struggled to find the petty cash box to pay the milkman!

As far as her private life was concerned, it was exactly that.

Boyfriends? No.

Girlfriends? Definitely not.

Hobbies? Whist, bridge and walking. DCI Lolly made a note to seek out her card playing partners.

Her only extravagance and apparent pride and joy appeared to be a brand new Audi Coupe GT.

The two detectives continued with their routine questions which gave them few clues they felt were worth following up.

"Has she fallen out with anyone in the office recently or had a row?" asked DS Walker.

He was desperately searching for some lead.

Tim took his time before answering.

"She fell out with everybody and nobody just about every day of the week – and that included me. She was just that sort of bossy woman. But as for a full scale office row, no, people didn't dare! Having said all that, I will miss her. During my editorship I had come to rely on her. She was my rock in this place, albeit a pain in the ash tray some days"

Tony Morrisey was also recalled for a second interview. He told the two detectives virtually the same story as his editor and said he would also miss the office 'battle axe'.

"I think every newspaper office needs an Edna Sparrow to ensure some sort of order," he told them. "Journalists are a pretty disorganised bunch who need their noses wiped fairly regularly if they are to survive. I hate to think what the state of their homes is like. Edna kept the office sane."

DS Walker had seen the news room six months previously when being interviewed for a story about a missing girl. He could only hazard a guess about how much of a mess it would have been in if Edna Sparrow had not kept an eye on things. There was so much paper on the floor one match could have set the whole building alight.

He asked Tony: "Have you any idea why she came back so hastily from holiday? Did she give you any hint as to her reasons? If she hadn't she might still be alive today and resting up."

Tony couldn't give him a satisfactory answer.

"I was surprised myself because there was no real need for her to come back. OK, the contents of her filing cabinet were all over the news room floor, but it didn't take all that long to pick everything up and drop it into large boxes we already had stored at the back of the building. She insisted on taking the boxes home, saying she would get more done there in the peace and quiet."

The detective pressed him a bit further.

"Was she in the habit of coming in to work during her holidays – travelling quite a distance from somewhere she was staying?"

He knew of other lonely singles who missed the companionship and purpose they found at work; after a few days on holiday they were so bored with their own company they popped into their work places for a chat.

"No," said Tony. "In fact it was the exact opposite. She made it quite clear she should never be disturbed while on holiday, or when she took a day off, unless it was an extreme emergency. I think there would have had to have been a murder before......."

He trailed off when he realised what he was saying.

So why did she come back this time just because the office had been burgled, thought the two detectives? The answer to that question was something that puzzled them long after Tony returned to the news room to keep tabs on his reporting team. They felt it was the key to Edna Sparrow's murder.

"Get somebody to go round to her house and bring in those boxes," said DCI Lolly.

"They will have to be given back to the Herald eventually, but I think we ought to look at what they hold before we hand them over. I am sure after we have finished with them Mr Chinnery would like to be the first person in this building to see what they contain."

Nearly every member of the Herald's staff was interviewed during the rest of Friday. Some interviews were very short, particularly with the younger members of the advertising staff. Nobody could offer any suggestion or clue as to why the editorial secretary had been murdered, or why she was in the office on her own at eight o'clock on a Thursday evening, unless it was to start repairing the damage done to her filing system.

"It just won't do," said DCI Lolly to his colleague before they departed for their homes. "It doesn't make any sense. Then again, most murders never do."

CHAPTER SIXTEEN

Edna Sparrow's body was removed from the news room by a firm of local undertakers. It would remain with them as evidence until the coroner released it.

Dick watched the hearse pull away. He was having difficulty in concentrating on anything meaningful. He would have liked to have sat in on the individual meetings DCI Lolly and DS Walker were holding with Tim Fletcher and his team, but there was no way that was going to happen. He watched as one by one they trooped in and out of the editorial department, which was still out of bounds. They looked a sorry lot.

Tim gave him Edna's personnel file and after a couple of telephone calls he managed to trace an elderly aunt in a nursing home in Scotland and an old school friend in Devon. The aunt was in no fit state to really understand what she was told. The nursing home's matron said there was no way she would be able to travel to any funeral.

The friend was more helpful but said she had not seen Edna for six years despite living in the neighbouring county. Dick gave her telephone number to DCI Lolly. There was nothing in

Edna's desk drawers which gave a clue as to who she had stayed with in Hampshire. He assumed the police would discover that when they searched her house along with her will and an address book.

He felt drained, physically and emotionally and was glad when the time came for him to leave the office in a pool car and drive to Bodmin Parkway to pick up Mary. Apart from when he had visited her in hospital after she had been brutally attacked in Thurnham six years ago, he could not remember a time when he had been more pleased to see her.

"Welcome to your latest holiday destination," he said as she hugged him.

He picked up her case.

"Blimey, what have you got in here – the Crown Jewels?"

She gave him a dig in the ribs.

"A lady needs all her personal effects so she can look the best for her man, particularly when she will need to make an impression on his new colleagues."

He retrieved the situation.

"You make an impression on everyone you meet no matter what the circumstances."

It got him off the hook.

On the drive to the Royal Imperial Hotel he briefed her on all that had happened. She already knew some of it. After she had unpacked and taken in the exceptional view from their room, she sat him down on the bed and drew up a chair.

"Right, before we have dinner, I am going to interview you Mr Chinnery and find out just how much my shorthand speed has dropped since I became an editor. I will decide what is important and what is not for the stories you are expecting me to write by Monday tea-time."

He loved her. When she felt she had got it all down in her notebook they went to the hotel's main restaurant and had a sumptuous three course dinner, during which she told him: "If I see you ordering a full English breakfast while I am here, you are in big trouble!"

Frank Helliwell was a worried man. He had not yet been interviewed by the police, and hoped there might still be a chance he never would be, but Edna's murder on the same evening and possibly at the same time as they were due to have what was going to be a hostile meeting would definitely interest them. He had spoken to all six members of the press crew and they had been unanimous that if asked they would all say they had been too busy to notice anything unusual on Thursday evening.

He didn't want to go into work on Saturday morning, but it was his turn to do a half-day shift and he could not get out of it. He also feared that if he didn't turn up it would look suspicious. For the second night running he had not slept well and had ended up in the spare bedroom.

He arrived in his usual car parking slot at the same time as Rufus Jones.

*

The freelance reporter had spent all day Friday in his boat fishing. He had been totally out of touch with all that had happened at the Herald Express until he had called in at the Dog and Duck on Friday evening for something to eat and a couple of pints.

"Your paper been upsetting somebody?" the landlord had enquired as he pulled Rufus a pint of Hook Norton bitter. "You will have to watch your back until they catch him."

"I have no idea what you are talking about. Catch who?" he had asked.

The landlord had brought Rufus up to date. After a sausage and mash dinner the freelance reporter had done something he rarely did – he had refused a second pint and instead had headed for the Herald Express office. On arrival he had found six police cars all flashing their lights outside the main entrance and the building a hive of activity. A local television crew were filming outside. He had circled the car park and left as quickly as he had arrived.

When Frank and Rufus parked their cars next to each other the following morning it looked to the latter as though the same six police cars were still outside the main entrance, but the TV van was gone.

Rufus had made a few telephone calls on Friday evening which had provided him with a reasonable outline of what had happened in his absence. He did not mourn Edna's passing. They had never got on and her eyes seemed to follow him every time he went outside to smoke a cigarette or have any sort of break. She had queried several of his invoices and made him re-submit the number of hours he said he had worked some weeks.

He had felt humiliated when he was given that written warning and blamed her for the temporary end of his lucrative pre-publication scan of the free ads on all four papers produced at Broad Bottom.

"You look terrible," he told Frank.

"And a good morning to you too," snapped the normally affable production manager. "A bit early for you to be around on a Saturday morning isn't it?"

Rufus did not respond. The two men headed for separate doors.

A policeman stopped Rufus from entering the editorial department. Even when he insisted he needed his typewriter and a couple of notebooks he was firmly pointed towards the boardroom.

"I think you will find all you need in there, sir," the policeman politely but firmly told him.

Rufus had no choice but to comply. He opened the door and was pleasantly surprised to find the only other person in the room was a very attractive newcomer. She looked at him once, said "hello" and carried on typing.

"I suppose you are a temp standing in for our former editorial secretary?" he said.

Mary stopped typing. She hated to be disturbed when she was in full flow, but decided she should be polite – for a short time at least. She stood up, held out her hand and told him.

"No, I am Mary from the Torchester Evening Gazette. I have been seconded for as long as necessary to handle the murder stories because it was felt everyone here would be too upset and would not want to do them."

She deliberately did not give him her surname.

Rufus held her hand far longer than ordinary protocol required and also stood far too close to her.

"Nice to meet you, Mary, perhaps we can share a few stories and get to know each other better over a drink tonight?"

"And why should I want to do that?" she asked.

"Because you are on your own a long way from home and it can be quite lonely at the weekend without somebody by your side."

Blimey, she thought, *and there's me thinking they are a tad slow in this part of the world.*

"You don't want to be on your own at some cold B and B. I have plenty of room at my cottage."

She knew exactly what he meant.

"I don't think so," was her tart reply.

And just to make sure he got the message she brought the heel of her right shoe down on his foot.

Rufus grunted and grabbed her none too gently by the arm. He was about to say something when he found himself being lifted off the ground and propelled towards the door by someone behind him. Dick Chinnery had one hand behind his collar and the other inside the top of his trousers.

A startled policeman did not interfere as Dick frog-marched the reporter out of the front door.

"You are the worse sort of creep Jones. Your employment with this company is over and if I have anything to do with it you won't work for any other newspaper. I will have your belongings packed up and sent to you next week along with one week's money, which is exactly one week more than you deserve. Now get out of my sight before I do something to you this policeman might find difficult to ignore."

Rufus stumbled and grazed both knees. It had been a long time since anyone had manhandled him. He was quick to respond.

"You will regret this Mr High and Mighty. I am a member of An Gof and we have a way of dealing with people like you down here. Wait you see."

Dick had no idea what An Gof was or anything about Rufus Jones' involvement. He laughed, turned his back and set off to make sure his wife was alright. Out of the corner of his eye he spotted a smiling Lulu Popplewell who had just parked her car. He simply nodded in her direction and she returned the gesture.

"I have dealt with his sort before," said Mary. "But thank you for being my knight in shining armour. I thought you were going to punch him. I am glad you didn't because I think that policeman would have had to arrest you, and that wouldn't do at all because I would have had to do the story."

Soon after she was introduced to both Tim Fletcher and Tony Morrisey, but again she did not give her surname – and they didn't ask.

"Did I see Rufus just leaving," enquired Tim.

"Permanently. Mr Jones has had his employment with this company terminated."

Editor and chief reporter gave him blank looks.

"Did you know he was a member of some organisation called An Gof?"

For a moment Tim looked startled, but soon composed himself.

"They are some sort of nationalist group who believe Cornwall should be a separate country. Trouble-makers and no-gooders in the main, but they have had their violent moments."

Dick looked up to the heavens for inspiration.

"Do tell me more, Tim. I can't wait to be educated."

The editor explained that it went back to a Cornish rebellion of 1497 against Henry VII which had been brutally suppressed. Nothing much had happened after that for nearly 500 years but in 1980 a group calling itself An Gof exploded a bomb at St Austell court. Since then tourist attractions had been targeted and on one occasion broken glass had been strewn across several local beaches to try and deter visitors.

"What nice people they must be – hoping to hurt children playing on a beach," said Dick. "And one of their number was in your news room gathering intelligence all this time. Congratulations. I have never found a suspected terrorist in any of my news rooms before."

The editor was lost for words. Dick didn't give him the chance to recover.

"If you come into my temporary office I will tell you why Mr Jones will never cross the threshold of this office again and what needs to be done to make sure we stay the right side of employment legislation so he has no chance of winning a payout at an industrial tribunal. And don't worry, you have my permission to employ another freelance and you have Mary as an extra so it shouldn't cause you too many problems this week."

My world has turned upside down in too short a time, thought Tim. He could only ponder on what might happen next.

*

The office was so quiet on a Saturday morning that Mary was able to produce three long stories. She got tribute quotes out of both Tim and Tony praising Edna's long service at the Herald Express, while over the phone a clearly upset Harvey Fairbanks provided a deeper insight into the sort of person she was. He agreed to write a first person piece for next Friday's paper which would freshen up the story. After four hours she felt there was little else she could do until Monday.

Dick kept out of her way. He decided the best use he could make of his time was to man the telephones and head off any interruptions. He had always found it rather amusing what the public demanded from their local newspaper. One man wanted to know if the Herald could tell him the time of the last bus from Truro to Broad Bottom; another asked about the price of a house featured in that week's Herald Express and whether he thought the vendor would accept a lower price? He had to tell one woman who had a sick dog he did not know the name of a local vet who was open on a Saturday or the duty chemist. Then he fielded the best one of all.

"Do you know the name and number of an emergency weekend plumber?"

He didn't, but suggested the caller tried directory enquiries.

"But I am directory enquiries," came the reply.

By the time Mary said she could write no more he had had enough of answering the phone. He wondered if such calls came in every day of the week. He thought Lulu would know.

"You had the polite ones," she said.

"By the way, thank you for getting rid of that dreadful Rufus Jones. Several of my girls will be delighted when I tell them on Monday."

And with that Mr and Mrs Chinnery left to have a light lunch at a pub three miles away which came highly recommended by Tony who thought the new reporter and her boss were "very chummy" when he was quizzed by Tim.

CHAPTER SEVENTEEN

Content in each other's company after they had eaten more than they had intended, the Chinnerys went back to the Royal Imperial where Mary changed her shoes. Because it was such a beautifully sunny afternoon they decided a good walk would do both of them a world of good. Dick led her through the hotel gardens, past the miniature golf course and out onto a broad beach which was busy, but not uncomfortably so.

They enjoyed an ice cream, climbed up some steep steps and found themselves in the Fairbanks Memorial Park. Dick rightly guessed that Harvey's ancestor had given the land to the town in the 19th century on condition it was used for recreational and sporting purposes. A large sign contained both the history of the town and that of the Fairbanks family. Smuggling appeared to have been the main local industry well into the 20th century.

A bowls match was in progress. The benches they sat on opposite the bowling green enabled them to give their by now aching feet a rest.

"Do you remember last year when Shaldon Bowls Club put up posters advertising their open day and didn't notice the printer had inserted an 'e' into the word 'bowls'?"

She gave one of her girly giggles.

"I bet they wouldn't have spotted it down here," he added.

"Oh, that's rather unkind," she remarked. "You are too judgemental Mr Chinnery."

They continued their walk and came up to a large board and fence which told them they could not walk any further in their intended direction because it was the property of Broad Bottom Tennis Club. Dick was about to turn round and find a different route back to the hotel when some instinct made him read the board and the poster inside a glass covered frame.

It nearly spoiled his afternoon.

"What's up?" said Mary.

"I suspect I have just found out about another scam which will make next week interesting. Jack Wilde won't believe me."

On the way back to the hotel he told her all about it.

✳

In London Ryan Johnston and Marie-Clementine Dubois were having a delightful early Saturday evening dinner in a quiet back street Kensington restaurant. She had just ordered a Dover sole and he a rare to medium steak when she noticed someone she knew as Jason Pearce, chairman of British Aerospace, approaching their table. He was accompanied by two men wearing long coats who she instinctively knew were either plain clothes policemen or representatives of a more senior organisation. She feared it was the latter.

The three men approached their table, showed their identity cards and asked Ryan and Marie-Clementine to quietly follow them. She glanced at the first card and saw the name Arthur Nightingale. It meant nothing to her, but she knew he had been her guest at the last House of Commons lunch.

She was about to protest, but then dismissed the thought. She had been brought up better than to engage in an unseemly row in front of Saturday night diners.

Ryan froze. At first he didn't think he could get up out of his seat, the shock was so great. He was too stunned to say or do anything. Within a matter of seconds their coats had been collected and to all intents and purposes nothing of note had occurred in the restaurant.

Two cars were waiting outside. A traffic warden who had tried to slap parking tickets on them had been given short shrift a few minutes earlier.

The restaurant returned to normal except for the now empty table. The only person who wondered what had happened was a bemused waiter who when he came up from the cellar was surprised to find the couple who had ordered an expensive bottle of red wine were no longer to be seen.

There was further disappointment for the waiter and the restaurant's manager. A Russian couple who were halfway through their main course asked for their bill – immediately.

"My wife is not well. We have to go. The food is fine – my wife is not" was the only explanation forthcoming.

They left in a taxi soon after for a 'safe house' two miles away where on a secure line they reported what had happened to Ryan Johnston and Marie-Clementine Dubois and awaited further orders.

Sunday was another beautiful day in Cornwall. Hadn't she read in the Poldark novels that it rarely rained during the summer months? Mary didn't believe that. After breakfast they took the pool car and headed to St Ives, but it was full to overflowing. It took them an hour to drive round the town twice and realise there wasn't anywhere they could park and too many people were packed into too small an area. They took the main road out and went to nearby Carbis Bay where they found a car park near the beach. Mary dipped her toes in the water and was surprised how warm it was, while Dick found a spot out of the wind and attempted without much success to read the broadsheet Sunday Times.

They tried hard not to talk about work, but on the way back to the Royal Imperial Dick said: "Tomorrow when he you have written all you can about Edna's murder, I don't want you to head back to Thurnham just yet. Is that alright with you?"

It was more than alright. The last thing she wanted to do now was to leave him. Anyway she didn't fancy a seven hour train journey via London on her own.

On Monday morning there was some good news for the Broad Bottom Herald Express. DCI Lolly said the editorial team and Tim Fletcher could have their offices back. From now on the investigation would be conducted at the police station a mile away. He had a private chat with Dick before he left.

"This is not for publication, but so far we have hit a brick wall. What I find puzzling is why Miss Sparrow came back in such a hurry from her holiday. There was no need. From all accounts she was more agitated than usual; one reporter said he had never seen her so obviously out of control."

Dick agreed. From the limited experience he had of her habits, he thought she was a woman who was always in control and let everybody else know it.

"We are not ruling anything out, but I have a feeling somebody in this building knows far more than they are letting on. We need a break. By the way, I hear you have given Mr Jones the boot. Not before time in my opinion. We have refused to have any dealings with him after he broke an embargo we placed on a story last year."

It was further confirmation, not that Dick needed it, that his decision to get rid of the reporter was the correct one. He had no time for local newspaper journalists who acted like some of their national counterparts when it suited them and brought everyone into disrepute. When a newspaper was taken into the police's confidence and agreed to hold back publication of a story for whatever period of time was agreed between them, it was an act of faith and trust. It was his experience that there was generally a very good reason for having a police embargo in place.

DCI Lolly added: "Just one word of warning though before I leave you – a murderer is still at large. I understand you are not the most popular visitor to this part of Cornwall."

Dick raised his eyebrows, but did not comment.

"One of my junior officers was in his local pub last night and your name cropped up. A party of non-too-quiet Herald Express employees were talking about all the changes you have made and some, who probably had had too much to drink, were rather unkind about you."

It did not come as any surprise and was nothing new given his job – he had sacked far too many lazy journalists to believe he was universally popular.

He knew the detective was giving him the gentlest of warnings to take care until Edna Sparrow's killer was found.

"People do stupid things when they feel their way of life is threatened by an outsider. Just be careful, that's all. One murder in this backwater of the county is more than enough for me to be going on with."

Dick realised that while it was an obvious warning any policeman would give him considering all the circumstances, it was also a wise and friendly one aimed at him personally; he realised he and his wife ought to heed it.

The detective headed for the door, but turned before leaving.

"For what it is worth, I hope you do shake up the Herald Express. It is not the paper it was five years ago," he said.

*

An hour later after the reporters had carried their typewriters and other equipment back to the news room, DS Walker turned up with the remaining boxes they had removed from Edna Sparrow's home containing documents which had been strewn over the news room floor during the burglary.

"You might find a few items in this little lot very interesting," was all the detective would say.

Dick put the boxes on the boardroom table and waited for Mary to join him. He had another job to do before he could start trying to make some sense of the editorial secretary's files. He said good morning to Lulu Popplewell, walked through to the news room and then into the editor's office. He shut the door behind him.

"I had a very interesting walk on Saturday through the Fairbanks Memorial Park. I am not going to beat about the bush because I don't have the time, but how come you advertise tennis lessons on days when by any reasonable assumption you should be working here?"

Tim Fletcher's face flushed. He didn't know what to say, but he knew his worst fears when he first heard about the newspaper's change of ownership had just been confirmed.

"I don't care what you do in your own time, but I am getting really fed up of discovering one thing after another about you and your fellow journalists. Did Mr Fairbanks know you were short-changing him?"

Tim broke his silence.

"Harvey avoided confrontation if he could help it."

"Then you had better listen to what I am going to say very carefully because if there is one thing my managing director and I don't hold back on when necessary it is confrontation."

For the next few minutes Dick spelt out the hours Tim could offer his tennis lessons to the general public with the caveat that even then the Herald Express had to come first if his presence was needed for anything to do with his work.

"There is one other thing we ought to clear up. I cannot do anything about the free advertising I suspect you have been getting for your tennis lessons because what deals you struck with Harvey Fairbanks and his managers prior to the takeover are not my concern. I suggest you hastily pay for any such adverts you have had the last three weeks since the Thompson Group took ownership, minus, of course, the usual staff discount."

"I am going to put all this down in writing for you. To save your blushes with the others I shall have the letter typed by my secretary in Torchester, but be under no illusion that if, when I go back to Essex, I discover you have slipped back into your old ways I shall catch the next flight and personally kick you out of the door."

Tim believed him.

"Now is there anything else I should know about the way this newspaper is run, or will I have to find it out for myself in the coming days?"

Tim took his time before he answered.

"I think you ought to know about Tony Morrisey's arrangement."

Dick groaned. *What now*? he thought. *Another scam? No wonder the Cornish want independence from the rest of the UK!*

"And what arrangement would that be?"

Tim again took his time.

"It concerns the woman who writes the Tufty Club column for under 10s."

Dick stared in disbelief. This was a new one even for him. Jack and Mary would love it.

"He has two hours off every Friday to collect her copy from her home two miles away. She doesn't charge as much as she used to as long as they have some fun."

"Some arrangement!" uttered a nearly incredulous Dick.

"Does he come back to the office with a smile on his face?"

"Most weeks," answered Tim.

"It pleases everyone and helps my freelance budget."

Enough was enough – he couldn't take any more of this.

"Anything else?" enquired Dick.

Tim shook his head.

"Let me know if you think of anything because I have to write a report for head office and I wouldn't want to leave out one word of this."

And with that he felt he had said enough – for the time being.

When Dick got back to the safety of the boardroom Mary was waiting for him. She had finished for the time being all she could write about Edna Sparrow's murder. He could not resist telling her about the Tufty Club. She laughed until her sides ached; tears rolled down her face. Every time she tried to speak the words would not come out. He made her a cup of tea so she could calm down.

"I would love to see Jack Wilde's face when you tell him," she said.

"Oh, and by the way, the sub-editors asked for my surname for the by-line on tomorrow's stories. I have given them my maiden name – Lynch. Let's see how long it is before they cotton on we are married."

They spent the rest of the afternoon sorting through Edna's boxes; it was not an easy task. Lulu Popplewell came in for a brief chat about one particular advertiser, which gave Dick the opportunity to ask if she knew of any special arrangement with regard to Tim's tennis school.

"It didn't take you long to find that out," she said. "When first I came here from Barnstaple I spoke to Mr Fairbanks about it, but he said it was ok for him to get free advertising. Since then we have never sent him an invoice."

Dick now felt he understood what sort of person Harvey Fairbanks was – kind and generous to all and sundry, but hardly a good businessman.

"From now on you will invoice Mr Fletcher on a monthly basis, minus the usual ten per cent staff discount," he said.

Lulu scribbled his instruction on a piece of paper.

"By the way three of my staff have already told me how pleased they are that Rufus Jones no longer works here," she added while heading for the door. "I think they were on the verge of lodging a sexual harassment complaint."

That was the last thing Dick wanted to get involved with at the moment. *Be grateful for small mercies*, he thought.

"She's OK," said Mary when Lulu left.

Dick had come to the same conclusion.

The break the police sought with regard to Edna Sparrow's murder came less than 24 hours later.

CHAPTER EIGHTEEN

When the Tuesday edition of the Herald Express went on sale the extra copies Dick had insisted should be printed were eagerly snapped up by newsagents. The failure of the police to get anywhere near solving what was now openly being described as murder meant there were no restrictions on what the paper could print.

The landlord of the Red Lion in Piddle Wood collected a bundle of papers every day from his local newsagent who could not find anyone to do a delivery round. He slotted the Daily Telegraph into the wall holder, then the Daily Mail, followed by the Sun. When he glanced at the Herald Express he realised the woman who everyone had been talking about in his bar for the last few days was the same one who had caused such a fuss only a couple of days before she had been murdered. He didn't put the paper on display.

The landlord's call when it came in to police headquarters sent DCI Lolly and DS Walker rushing for their coats. They interviewed him 40 minutes later.

"She was quite worked up about something," he told them. "She had a right go at the man she was with. They sat over in that corner," he said pointing to a window seat.

"Did they arrive together?" asked DCI Lolly.

"I don't think so. No, they bought their drinks separately and she left on her own."

The senior detective took it slowly. It was something he had had to learn the hard way when he first came to Cornwall from the West Midlands.

"Have you any idea what they were arguing about?" he enquired.

The landlord rubbed his chin and pondered for 20 seconds.

"I think he accused her of something, but we were busy and I only got a few snatches of their conversation. It was only when she got up to leave that most of us found out she was very angry. She gave him quite a mouthful. You would not have thought such a well dressed middle-age woman would have known such language."

DCI Lolly disagreed. He had met quite a few well dressed middle-age women who could use language which would not have been out of place in a dockyard. Their appearances had not seemed to make any difference to what had come out of their mouths when they were roused.

He realised he had got as much information as he was going to get from the Red Lion's landlord.

"Just one more question before I get my colleague to take down a description of the man she was with. Did she mention his name?"

"Frank. He was a Frank. I am sure of that. I remembered it because my brother's name is Frank"

When they left the Red Lion the two detectives headed straight for the Herald Express.

Dick also received some good news on Tuesday morning. Richard Orange phoned him to say he had received an unexpected telephone call from Archibald Lang who had spoken to the Chief Constable of the East Anglian Police Force the day before. It appeared that Ryan Johnston would not be proceeding with his defamation action against the Broad Bottom Herald Express.

"When Mr Lang asked for an explanation and said he would need something in writing from his client before he could terminate his involvement, he was told that would be forthcoming in due course, but he might serve his client's interests better if he made one of his team available to represent Mr Johnston when he was interviewed under caution at Torchester police station at 2pm today"

Richard added: "From what I have since discovered it was such a shock the elderly solicitor stumbled, banged his head on the side of his solid oak desk and suffered a cut which needed six stitches. He eventually managed to buzz his secretary who came in to find him slumped in a chair holding a blooded handkerchief to his head. That is why he didn't ring me until now."

"Has he recovered?" asked Dick out of politeness.

Richard assured him that Archibald Lang was made of the right sort of stern stuff.

"Before he was taken to hospital to get patched up he called in a junior partner, told him what he needed to do and then insisted on being allowed to sit back in his chair to try and work out what the Deputy Chief Constable could possibly have done wrong."

They don't make them like that any more, thought Dick.

"His secretary told me that when they eventually got him out of his office and on his way to hospital all he kept muttering was '*what a strange world we live in.*' While he was waiting to be stitched he had found a pay phone to reassure his partner, Marshall Hart, he would be fine and be back in the office the next day."

*

When the police car pulled up outside the front door of the Herald Express Dick nudged Mary.

"This could be interesting" he said as he pointed out of the window.

The detectives didn't bother to sign the visitors' book on the reception counter. They had no time for such formalities. Dick met them at the boardroom door and ushered them in.

"Have you got anyone working here called Frank?" asked DCI Lolly.

Dick uncovered the staff list from a pile of papers he had kept separate from those in Edna Sparrow's boxes.

"It looks like we have two – a Frankie Swann who works in the advertising department and Frank Helliwell our production manager."

"If Frankie wears a skirt then we can discount her," said DS Walker.

"Can we use this room to have a chat with Mr Helliwell?"

It was more of a demand than a request.

Dick nodded his agreement and went out to fetch his production manager. He found him talking to one of the men making up pages for the Crackington Gazette.

"Two men want to have a talk with you in the boardroom," Dick told him in as friendly manner as he could muster.

"Sorry, but there is too much for me to do here – ask them to come back another day. I presume they are ink salesmen?"

Dick led Frank away and out of the earshot of anyone else.

"They are policemen and I don't think they will be happy to wait until later in the week."

It was a good job Dick was holding Frank's arm because there was a distinct buckling of his legs.

When he reached the boardroom with Frank alongside him, Dick discovered Mary had already left; she had decided her presence would not be required and had already carried out a diplomatic retreat towards the advertising department.

Frank was introduced to DCI Lolly and DS Walker after which Dick left to join her.

"Let's ask Lulu if she knows a cafe with a good view that's not too far away and go and have a coffee," she said

The advertising manager duly obliged them. She said she had the cafe's telephone number if either of them was needed more quickly than she guessed they would be.

*

The cafe was not busy and indeed had fabulous views of the beaches below and coastline. They asked what coffees were available and the waitress told them, without displaying any semblance of a smile, that she served two sorts – black and white. Dick could not resist teasing her.

"Can you do me a cappuccino and my wife a latte?"

The waitress gave him a look of contempt.

"If you want either of those you will have to go to Penzance. And even then you might not be lucky"

"Two white coffees, then, with hot milk please."

Mary had another fit of the giggles.

"You are naughty," she chided him. "But tell me: what are contra deals? I came across the term while searching through one of the boxes"

Dick had another of those sinking feelings of which he had had far too many since he came to Cornwall. He explained what he believed they were.

"It's a bit like old-time bartering before coins became popular. You did a job for someone and they gave you a chicken or some vegetables; it worked for both parties and is still done today in some new age communities in this country and many Third World countries."

She spotted his worried look.

"It's OK I am not going to give you another headache. I understand now the meaning behind some of the records I have been viewing. It appears that Tim's predecessor as editor did quite a few contra deals. He got a new kitchen done on the cheap by arranging for the firm to get a 50% reduction in its advertising bills over a three year period. He did other contra deals with various advertisers as and when he needed something."

Dick looked at her in astonishment.

"That is crooked," he said. "We will never know one half of what went on under old man Fairbanks' nose. I bet that if we had the time or the inclination we would discover he was taken to the cleaners by quite a few people. I wonder if Henry Thompson bought him out to do him a favour and save himself from himself?"

The good news, she told him, was that so far there was no evidence that Tim Fletcher was pulling the same scam. The bad news was that Edna Sparrow had somehow managed to keep a record of many other questionable dealings along with numerous juicy tit-bits about various individuals.

"Some of it is very personal," she added. "It was all kept in that filing cabinet which was targeted by whoever broke in the other day. Once we have the complete picture of what that filing cabinet contained we will have to tell those two nice policemen what we have discovered, although judging by what they said when they returned the boxes they already know quite a bit."

The coffee when it arrived was just about drinkable.

There was no need for Lulu to call them back in a hurry. They were able to finish their drinks and be back in the office well before Frank's interview was over.

DCI Lolly asked the production manager to sit opposite them. He explained that at this stage they were still making many enquiries and this was just one of them.

Frank looked nervous before they even started the serious questioning.

"Have you any idea why anyone should want to murder your friend Edna?" was their opening gambit.

Frank shook his head.

"Well she wasn't a friend as such. When you work on a newspaper you have to have a professional relationship with key people in every department."

He had given DCI Lolly an opening.

"You say she wasn't a friend, yet you had midweek meetings with her in pubs not far away."

Frank felt as though somebody had just punched him in the stomach.

"And according to our information one such meeting took place only two days before she was murdered when the pair of you exchanged – for the moment let's say – harsh words."

The game was up, thought, Frank, they know too much.

He clenched his hands and then fought back. He could not help himself.

"If you think I murdered her you must be mad!"

The detectives were too experienced not to have heard that statement many times before.

"So what was the purpose of that particular get-together if you weren't friends? Did your wife know about it?"

That was one straight answer he could give them without faltering.

"Yes, she did. She knew all about it. I don't go anywhere without her knowing exactly where she can find me"

210

That would have to be checked, thought DS Walker, who took up the questioning while his colleague watched.

"Then tell us what the meeting was all about if it was all above board. And why couldn't it have taken place at work rather than in a village pub?"

For the next forty five minutes the two detectives sat and listened, partly amused and party disgusted at the deceit, as Frank explained exactly what he and the six men who printed the Herald Express had been doing to supplement their earnings for the last ten years.

"And what was Edna Sparrow's role?" asked DCI Lolly when Frank had finished.

"She kept all the records of who had done what and the money the estate agents owed us. I am sure that you will find she has a bank account set up solely to handle all payments."

They would have to speak to the other six men involved, but they had no reason to doubt they had been told the truth.

"What was the row in the Red Lion about then?"

Dick prevaricated.

"We had a golden rule that any discussion about what we were doing should not be held in the Herald Express office in case anyone not involved in our little business set-up overheard us. I represented the men in such meetings. They were always about the money we were getting or any problems we had encountered. Edna used to get a bit upset if I as much hinted she might not be treating us fairly."

DCI Lolly was not satisfied, but let it pass for the moment.

"Why did you feel she was not handling things well? She appears to have been a very competent woman."

"It was minor stuff really about the paperwork."

Frank left that comment up in the air.

"For the record, where were you on the night of the murder?" asked DS Walker.

"I was here with the rest of the lads over-seeing the final print run. I never get home on any Thursday before 9pm, even on a good week."

With that they let him go back to work. His hands were shaking.

CHAPTER NINETEEN

DCI Lolly and DS Walker went to find Dick and Mary. They were two of the few people in Cornwall who knew the editorial director and his female reporter were married, so they weren't surprised when on their return to the boardroom Dick told them they would both like to hear whatever the police felt it was alright to tell them.

The two detectives reckoned that by now the landlord of the Red Lion had probably told all and sundry what he knew and how he was playing a major part in helping the police catch a killer.

DCI Lolly also knew it would be exaggerated a hundred times over the next few days when the Red Lion's regulars passed it on. He half expected to hear rumours of a mass murderer at large before long!

"Do you know about the business your printers are running on the side?" he asked.

"No," replied Dick, "but after what I have discovered since I came down here - what seems like a lifetime ago - nothing would surprise me."

It was left to DS Walker to educate the pair of them.

"They run a photograph service on behalf of most of your estate agents at rates no professional photographer with the usual overheads can match. The majority of the pictures appearing in estate agents' advertising in your four papers are done by your own staff who sneak off every Tuesday and snap most of them."

No wonder they didn't want to print anything on that day, thought Dick. *It explains everything. I bet they have been using our dark room materials as well when it suits them.*

He made a note to check.

"It does not take a lot of photographic skill to take a picture of a house," continued DS Walker. "Miss Sparrow kept records for them and took a slice of the action for her troubles."

"Why do you think she and Frank had a very public row in the Red Lion?" asked Mary, her nose twitching.

"That is something we are going to find out when we interview Mr Helliwell a second time quite soon, probably tomorrow" replied DCI Lolly. "Before that, however, we need to make a few more enquiries.

And with that they were on their way.

When Frank returned to the production department after his grilling he felt he had to tell the others about his interview with the two detectives, even though it broke their golden rule of never discussing business affairs within the Herald Express building. As was usual for a Tuesday only three of them were cleaning the press. Jonny Grayson could tell right away something was wrong; Frank took him to one side.

"The police know everything about our deal with the estate agents and by now will probably have informed Mr Chinnery. The game is up unless we can come up with some other way of operating. We urgently need to tell the others who are currently scattered round the district taking photographs. I suggest you and I get on the phone as soon after five o'clock as we can and arrange for us all to meet in the Chequers two hours later."

Jonny agreed it was the only sensible thing they could do. He wasn't sure how they should proceed, though. Neither did Frank!

There was no question about the first task Dick decided to prioritise on Wednesday morning when he confidently expected everyone working on the press would have made yet another miraculous recovery from their 'sickness bug'. He

215

strode into their domain, called them together and told them their futures.

After outlining what he knew about their operation, and that as far as Tuesdays were concerned it was well and truly at an end, he surprised them.

"I admire your entrepreneurial flair, I really do. And after I have given it some thought I have decided there is nothing I can do about anything you do in your own time. Good luck to you!"

Frank Helliwell and Jonny Grayson looked at each other. This was unexpected and not at all what they had thought would be the case when they had sat glumly over their pints in the Chequers the night before unable to agree a single course of action.

"But ....." Dick let the one word hang in the air for effect.

"But if one of you ever again reports sick on a Tuesday – or any other day of the week for that matter - without a very good reason, you won't get through the door the next day."

Jonny Grayson tried to interrupt him, but Dick was not going to let any of them say anything until he had finished. Then there would be time for questions – if they dared.

"I have two other options. The first is to sack all of you and hire a new press crew. I wouldn't do that today. I would do it behind your backs, like you did to Harvey Fairbanks. The second option is to move printing elsewhere. The Western Morning News have a giant press at Plymouth. I am sure they would love to get the contract to print our titles."

None of them could look him in the eye.

"Finally, at least for the moment, you are going to confess what you did in writing. I will get the necessary letters drawn up for you to sign. They will be kept in Torchester, but your new managing director will know about them."

"Oh, and before I forget, I am going to check the dark room and get someone from head office to come down and go through all invoices for photographic materials. When the audit is complete all of you can expect a hefty bill you will be able to pay from your extra earnings."

There were no questions.

He was about to leave them with the imminent task of plating up the press when he remembered something else.

"I almost forgot. The police want to interview all of you again because it now appears you and a few van drivers were the only people in the building along with the killer when Edna Sparrow was murdered. They think you might have seen something which could help them."

Frank's hands started to shake again.

Dick was wrong about who was on site at the time of the murder, as he discovered later. He returned to the boardroom where Mary was still sorting through Edna Sparrow's files.

"I think I am getting somewhere at last," she said. "Give me another hour then I think we ought to have a chat and decide what to do."

He knew better than to press her further.

His phone rang. Lulu Popplewell wanted to see him. He got several friendly greetings when he walked through the advertising department – the bran tub was proving a great success. The big board on the wall indicated it was going to be another bumper week for advertising revenues on all four papers.

Lulu's office at the far end had glass windows so she could see out. He could see she was stood up waving him in.

"I am sorry if you might feel I have delayed too long, but I don't believe Frank is a killer," she exclaimed.

Dick looked at her in amazement. Nobody had yet accused his production manager of anything.

"Who says he is?" he asked.

"On the night when Edna was murdered I returned to the office at eight o'clock to pick up my car and go home. One of the girls had invited me to dinner that night to meet her boyfriend. He lives in Bristol. They are getting married in a few months' time."

She paused to gather her thoughts.

"My car had a service that day so she and I left the office in her car - she brought me back after we had eaten. The garage left my keys under the front right tyre."

Dick wondered where all this was leading.

Lulu knew she needed to get to the point, but she wasn't finding it easy.

"It was parked at the side of the building – the side adjoining the kitchen. Apart from the strong lights in the production department and from the press room there was a light on in the kitchen. I saw Frank in there and he looked very agitated. I waved, but he must not have seen me because he didn't respond."

"He might have been making a drink," said Dick.

"No, he wasn't doing anything but pacing up and down. I had to clear some files on my back seat and before I left I looked up and saw him looking at his watch and walking back and forth."

Dick knew Lulu had no option but to tell the police what she had seen - the timing might be critical. He went back to the boardroom and rang DCI Lolly. It was a short conversation.

"It is time for us to clear out again," he told Mary when he put the phone down. "Fancy another coffee?"

This time, however, they knew they needed to stay in the building to await developments – the coffee was home made and far tastier. Once again they took over Lulu's office while she made herself as comfortable as possible in the boardroom and awaited her interviewers.

By the time the two detectives arrived the advertising manager had controlled some, but not all, of her nerves. She took them through the same story she had told Dick half an hour earlier. They did not interrupt her until they felt she was just about finished.

DCI Lolly asked her a few questions, including the all-important: "Why did you not come forward earlier?"

She apologised and explained how she had not realised the significance of what she had seen until later.

They were not happy, but they felt satisfied she was telling the truth.

When a clearly shaken Lulu returned to her own office Dick left her with his wife whom he knew would find the right words to calm her down. He headed to the boardroom because he knew who would be the next person the detectives would want to interview.

"Let me fetch him so as to cause the least amount of fuss," said Dick.

DCI Lolly agreed.

When he entered the production department Dick didn't head straight for Frank. Instead, he sought out his deputy.

"I am making you personally responsible for ensuring the papers get away on time today. Report directly to me if you encounter any problems," he said.

For a moment the deputy production manager considered asking for some sort of explanation - and then thought better of it.

Frank's legs didn't buckle this time when he was told he had to attend a second police interview – now. He had somehow expected it. He followed Dick through the news room and advertising departments and closed the boardroom door behind him.

The detectives didn't waste any time on preliminaries.

"Why didn't you tell us that at the time we believe Edna Sparrow was murdered you were not in the production department with the other members of staff?"

"I regret it now," he replied.

I bet you do, thought DS Walker, who was letting his boss do the interviewing.

"I advise you to think very carefully before you answer this question. Why were you in the kitchen pacing up and down and, from what we have been told, looking very agitated?"

Frank saw no reason not to tell them the truth. After all they already knew about the photographic business.

"I had set up a meeting with Edna. We had discovered she was not being honest with us about the money the estate agents were paying. She was taking a sizeable back-hander. But she didn't turn up."

"How did you find out about her deceit?" interrupted DS Walker.

"When the contents of her filing cabinet were spilled on the floor during the burglary two men from my department volunteered to help gather them up in order for the reporters to carry on working. It took them over an hour – everything went in four big boxes for someone else to sort out later. The last thing we needed was for the work flow to be halted. We discovered the truth then," said Frank.

"What would be your answer if I was to say that I suspect you did meet Edna that night as arranged, you had another row, she left to get something in the news room from her filing cabinet, you followed her, grabbed the tie on the reporter's desk and strangled her," said DCI Lolly.

Frank took a moment to understand he was being accused of murder.

"It simply isn't true," he responded.

"I think this conversation should be continued at Broad Bottom police station. Would you like to call your solicitor to meet you there?" asked the senior detective.

The Herald Express production manager didn't have a solicitor.

When Dick was informed that Frank was going to be taken away to be interviewed under caution and needed a solicitor, he was momentarily at a loss what to do. He and Mary watched as Frank was escorted into a waiting police car.

After watching the car leave, Dick snapped out of his trance and called in Tim Fletcher. The Herald's editor said he knew a solicitor who might be available at short notice.

Dick left him to sort it out while he rang Mrs Helliwell. When he told her the bad news, she immediately burst into tears. In between her sobs he advised her to contact a close friend to keep her company. He did not know what else to say.

CHAPTER TWENTY

After Dick managed to calm down Mrs Helliwell and assure her the company would give whatever help they could, he realised he had better ring Jack Wilde in Torchester; he didn't want him to hear about Frank's arrest from any third party. Henry Thompson would also have to be told. It wasn't every day that one of his employees was arrested for murder; although over the years a few had been done for drink-driving and one had served a short prison term for assaulting his wife.

"Every new day brings new excitement," said the managing director on being told the news. "Thank goodness you have Mary there to help you. Is there any other help we can give you at this end?"

Dick couldn't think of any.

"I didn't expect you to have so much fun when I sent you down to sleepy Cornwall," added Jack in an attempt to lighten the mood. "I understand the last time the locals got so excited was when they thought Napoleon was about to invade."

They spent a few minutes going over what had happened in the past 24 hours and sharing some thoughts. Dick knew his boss had a sharp mind and might possibly think of something he had missed, but he couldn't come up with anything, for the moment.

"It looks like you have all corners covered," was Jack's wry comment.

"By the way how is Mrs Chinnery enjoying Cornwall? Do you think she could come to like it?"

Dick was immediately on his guard.

"And what is behind that remark?" he said.

"Henry Thompson asked me yesterday how you were getting on and said that if you wanted to step up to managing director level the Cornwall job was yours. It will be a while before there is such a vacancy here - I have no intention of dying for many years unless you bump me off."

Dick had to laugh.

"You cunning old devil. No, a thousand times no. Not in a million years and not for a million pounds. Hang on, if that is the salary I might reconsider."

They both laughed. They were good friends as well as work colleagues.

"I had to ask, Dick. If you had changed your mind and now wanted the job and not said anything to me I would have regretted it. I will tell Henry he will have to continue his search."

Dick felt flattered, but no more than that. When he put the phone down Mary gave him one of her knowing looks.

"Are we millionaires then?" she enquired.

"Essex is far more appealing than Cornwall right now."

She gave him a big kiss. It was a good job nobody was looking through any of the windows.

Dick knew word of Frank Helliwell's arrest for Edna Sparrow's murder would spread like wildfire through the building. He gave it half an hour before he deliberately marched out of the boardroom and into the newsroom. He was not going to let them gossip at the expense of their next edition. The talking stopped the moment he arrived.

Tim Fletcher was sat at his own desk in his editor's office.

"You will have to be very careful what you carry in Friday's paper," Dick told him. "I hope I don't have to remind you there is not a lot you can write about Edna's murder now the case is active under that Contempt of Court Act they passed four years ago."

Tim did not react.

"There is nothing to stop you doing a fulsome obituary about Edna's life as long as you don't go into too much detail about her murder. Harvey Fairbanks has written a nice piece to go alongside what you can legally write. I presume you know what you can and cannot write about Frank's arrest?"

Dick was not reassured by Tim's response.

"Can I use a picture of him?" he asked.

Dick took a deep breath before he responded.

"I think I had better look at what you hope to print before you send it through to the production department; I have always found a second opinion is worth having when it comes to legal issues. And, no, you can't use a picture of him at this stage in case identification is an issue if it ever goes to a full trial."

"I don't think Frank is a murderer," remarked Tim, who seemed unable to string together more than a few words at a time, or did not want to.

For some reason he could not fathom, neither did Dick think Frank was a murderer.

His visits to the production department, press room and finally the advertising team were short and to the point.

The deputy production manager confirmed everything was on schedule. He said he had held a short meeting with all

Frank's staff and reminded them that everyone was innocent until proven guilty.

"It won't make much difference, but Frank deserves that," he said as Dick left him to get on with his busy schedule.

Lulu Popplewell's advertising reps were too busy trying to earn their bonuses to take much time out once the initial excitement had died down. There was no bran tub celebration this morning, though. Lulu thought the sound of cheering staff would send the wrong message and be disrespectful.

"Do you think he murdered her?" asked Lulu.

For the second time in the space of a few minutes Dick shook his head.

"I find it hard to believe, but the police would not have arrested him if they didn't have some evidence we don't yet know about."

And with that he left her to get on with selling the remaining advertising slots.

After Dick and Mary had munched on their sandwiches they decided to get some fresh air and take a thirty minute walk which took them off the industrial estate and onto a coastal path where they sat on a convenient bench for a few minutes.

"How are things back in Thurnham?" he asked. At this moment his home town seemed a million miles away.

"It has been another good week for cracking stories. Andrea is a good deputy. She likes to be in charge every now again, but as we know she cannot cope with the pressures of being the permanent number one."

She regaled him with what stories would appear and on which pages in that week's Standard. The page one splash was about a dog which had attacked a 10-year-old girl who was playing with a friend in the main Thurnham park. The girl had to have 30 stitches in her face.

"Her mum has asked the Standard help her start a national campaign for all dogs to be kept on leads when in parks," added Mary.

"I bet you get plenty of letters on that one," said Dick. "From both sides of the argument."

Experience had taught them that animal stories attracted the largest postbags and some of the fiercest local debates outside councils and hospitals putting up car parking charges.

He knew Mary prided herself on the number of letters the Standard received each week about stories which had appeared in previous editions, most of which she published.

"We now have a grotbusting officer," she said.

"A what?"

"Thurnham Council is asking home owners to repaint the outside of their homes or face legal action. It's all to do with trying to present a brighter image and improve the environment. Several people have received letters asking them to carry out a variety of repairs and paint their properties – or else! They aren't happy."

Dick wanted to know if it was legal. She assured him that it was under the Town and Country Planning Act 1947.

"Why don't you ring Andrea and get a reporter and photographer to take a look at the frontages of councillors' homes? It would make a good follow-up story if some of our civic leaders could benefit from a visit from their own grotbuster," he said.

"A brilliant suggestion, "said Mary.

She never resented it when he came up with a good idea; they were a team and a good one at that.

"Is there anything else worth telling me? You do realise this conversation is helping my sanity after all that has happened at the Herald Express?" he added.

Mary patted his hand. "There's one more you will like. An adventurous two-year-old Shaldon boy sparked a massive police hunt to find where he lived and who his parents were.

He had climbed out of his cot, opened a living room window and gone walkabout clad in only his blue and white pyjamas with his shoes on the wrong feet."

Dick did like it. He encouraged all his editors, Mary included, to find good human interest stories for page three to offset the large number of doom and gloom stories in the rest of their papers most weeks.

"Tell me more," he said.

She was happy to oblige. "He was found wandering the streets at 6.30am, but nobody knew who he was. The police took him back to their station where he tucked into a breakfast. It was only when his mother reported him missing two hours later that they were able to reunite them. The funny thing is he became so attached to one female officer he screamed when she had to attend to other duties."

Dick didn't need to ask if the Standard had got pictures of all the people involved.

"Another excellent page 3 for you then, but nothing will ever beat your story about the boy with size 18 feet," said Dick as they made their way back to the office. "Remind me of the details again."

She was happy to oblige. "You mean the Thurnham schoolboy who was banned from playing rugby because his feet were too large. There were no rugby boots big enough and he was not allowed to play in trainers. With his family's permission we took a photograph of his feet and used it full size alongside the story."

"That's the one. I remember it now. Didn't the national papers pinch your story and the next day a rugby boot maker in Northamptonshire offer to make him two personalised pairs?"

"Yes," said Mary. "I am glad to say his family gave us all the credit because our story was accurate."

✳

When they got back to the boardroom Dick was handed a message by the receptionist asking him to ring DCI Lolly immediately he returned. It was a courtesy call to inform him Frank Helliwell had been formally charged with the murder of Miss Edna Sparrow. He would appear in magistrates court that afternoon for an initial hearing when it was expected he would be committed to Truro Crown Court for a full trial.

"Is he likely to get bail?" asked Dick, but he knew what the answer would be before he asked the question.

"I don't think there is any chance of that given it is a murder charge, despite his previous good record," replied the detective.

Dick thanked him for keeping him informed. *I wish all policemen were like that*, he thought. He felt he ought to go and see Mrs Helliwell. Mary thought it a good idea ,but asked if he minded going alone because she needed to finish off her investigations into the contents of Edna's boxes.

Frank's wife had composed herself by the time her husband's temporary boss arrived on the doorstep of her modern three-bedroomed house on a small estate in the village of Little Bottom. She offered to make him a cup of tea and asked if he would like a biscuit, both of which he accepted because he knew it would help make her feel a little better.

"They won't let me see him yet," she said while pouring him his tea. "The only person who can talk to him is that solicitor you kindly provided. I don't know how we are going to pay his bill."

Dick reassured her that in the short term the company would take care of that. He quietly hoped Frank had saved some of the money he had earned from the photographic business, because if the case did go to Truro Crown Court a defence team would not come cheap.

He asked her if there was anything she needed. She shook her head.

"I will be fine. I did a shop this morning."

Dick was worried about her living on her own, particularly if the story attracted the national newspapers and they laid siege outside.

She was quick to reassure him.

"Although Frank and I have lived alone for several years we have a daughter who is packing a bag right now in London and will be here tonight," she said.

Dick knew it was better if he asked her some basic questions before the police did. It would prepare her for the scrutiny she might come under.

"Did you know Frank and Edna had occasional evening meetings?"

"Oh yes, there was no secret there. They needed to discuss a small business partnership they set up years ago with a few others. I never understood it, but it brought in some extra money and enabled us to move into this house two years ago."

Dick looked around – the house was immaculate. Even the cushions looked as though they were standing to attention.

She pre-empted his next question.

"And if you think for one minute there was any hanky-panky going on you would be quite wrong. I don't like speaking ill of the dead, but my Frank could not stand her. He would often come home after their meetings muttering about how difficult she was – and he was never home late."

Dick didn't like to tell her many a husband covered his tracks with a similar story.

At that moment he didn't care and it didn't seem to matter whether she knew her husband was part of the Tuesday scam which had been conducted behind Harvey Fairbanks' back for at least ten years.

There was nothing to be gained from him staying any longer than good manners required. He reassured her everything possible would be done to help Frank, but he told her she would need to be patient and should let the police do their job.

"He didn't kill anyone," she said as he left.

For the third time that day Dick had to agree. What puzzled him was why he did.

When he returned to the Herald Express office an excited Mary came out to meet him. She virtually manhandled him through the door.

"I am going to show you something very, very interesting and get you thinking."

And with that she pushed him into the boardroom.

CHAPTER TWENTY ONE

He plopped himself down in the nearest seat. He knew to shut up when his wife was as excited as this. There had been times when she had first become an editor when she had talked non-stop over the dinner table about a campaign she wanted to run or a page one splash.

"I have packed the vast majority of Edna Sparrow's files in three boxes on the floor."

He looked to where she pointed.

"When Tim Fletcher employs a new editorial secretary the two of them will have to load everything into that new editorial filing cabinet which arrived this morning. It's the contents I have put in the fourth box I want us to concentrate on."

He waited patiently for her to explain – he knew she would not be rushed.

"It hasn't been easy sorting through a mountain of stuff because of the sheer volume of paper thrown on the news room floor during the burglary. Given subsequent events I don't think the police are spending too much time trying to find the perpetrators of that particular incident."

Dick had come to the same conclusion.

"Whatever we might think about Edna Sparrow, she was very thorough and good at her job. If anything, she was too good!"

He knew she was building up to her main point.

"It was when I discovered what can only be described as personal papers that I realised she would have made a first class private detective. Among all the useless memos Tim Fletcher has sent out over the years and the replies to readers moaning about silly mistakes in the Herald Express, are isolated reports on the private lives of quite a few of her work colleagues."

She had Dick's full attention.

"But before I tell you more I must not forget the funnies because after what I tell you the time for laughter will be strictly limited. You wouldn't believe some of the errors Tim has had to correct in future editions."

Dick allowed her to educate him.

"There are the usual apologies for calling them the British Legion not the Royal British Legion and for calling the Queen Her Royal Highness instead of Her Majesty. But just imagine explaining how Western Super Mayor, Red Ruff and the Pharaoh Islands got past the sub-editors. My favourite has to be the week a reporter mis-read his shorthand and cycle paths became psychopaths."

Dick shared in her amusement, but he and Jack Wilde would not tolerate such errors in the future.

"We have all dropped the occasional brick at one time or another – we are human after all! Don't forget you wrote the headline '*Man trapped in Turkey at Christmas*'," he said.

"How could I ever forget when you keep reminding me? Anyway I digress. Now it is time for me to educate you about the serious stuff. The information she held on quite a few people is a veritable encyclopaedia of who on the Herald Express's staff is doing what and with whom in Broad Bottom, plus a few where, when and why-fors."

For once Dick really was amazed.

"You mean in this sleepy backwater of England there are all sorts of goings on which make for juicy reading?" he asked.

"It's no different from anywhere else, actually, "said Mary. "The difference is someone went to the trouble of putting it down in writing - and that someone was murdered. I think we may have stumbled on why she was murdered, but I am still not sure by whom. It is time you locked the boardroom door so we are not interrupted and read some of the stuff I have been pouring over these last few days."

"Ok. Let us stop for a few moments while I say hello to Ellen McCraken," he said.

Dick wanted to see her and apologise for the limited time he could spare her before she went back to Crackington.

"Stand guard," he told Mary. "I promise I won't be more than ten minutes."

She had heard that many times before.

Ellen was not too disappointed when he explained it had been a difficult day and he could not chat for very long. She assured him all was well on her two papers, that it had been a good week, that she didn't bring him problems but solutions and told him he really must visit her office when he could get away "because we have real coffee."

He liked her more and more and would have loved to have chatted longer, but he knew more important matters awaited him in the boardroom.

"I am back," he announced much to Mary's surprise exactly four minutes after he had left. "Let's start reading and making notes."

Between them they sorted what they thought was trivial such as far too many dubious expenses claims, office spats, Rufus Jones' failed attempts to chat up anyone in a skirt and

Tony Morrisey's confession that he smoked some illegal substance at university.

The editorial secretary had also kept a sort of diary on loose sheets of paper which recorded her feelings about people on any given day. Quite a bit of it was vitriolic.

"She does come across as a rather nasty piece of work," said Mary. "She seems to have been a bitter woman who did not have much good to say about anybody, past or present."

"You mean a right cow," interrupted Dick.

"She even had something on Harvey Fairbanks. It appears he had his way with a couple of the advertising girls when he was much younger."

Lucky devil," he sighed.

Mary gave him a sardonic look.

"Right, this is what I want us to look at together. It is the records she kept on every member involved in the estate agents' photographic scam."

Dick flicked through a sheaf of papers recording far more detail about Frank Helliwell and the press room crew than she had written about anyone else but Tim Fletcher.

"Interesting stuff, but hardly worth murdering someone for," said Dick.

"You are missing the point. One person's file is not there. Look again."

It took him a minute to realise there was nothing at all in Edna Sparrow's files about Jonny Grayson.

"Now that is very strange," said Dick. "The question is whether we tell anyone about what we have found, or in this case not found. Should I ring DCI Lolly and leave it with him or is it time we did some of our own detective work?"

They continued their reading uninterrupted, but it was not until they returned to the Royal Imperial that they agreed over dinner what they would do next. Back in their room they spent a further hour pondering over the right way to proceed and then finally decided they would sleep on it. If they still felt the same way tomorrow they would act decisively on their own.

Edna Sparrow's documents relating to several members of staff at the Herald Express stayed with them in their bedroom all night.

The next morning they were still of the same mind, but opted to wait 24 frustrating hours before putting their plan into operation. It was a calculated gamble, but they reasoned it was too hectic in the office on a Thursday for them to cause any major disruption that would threaten the entire production schedule on the busiest day of the week. On balance, they felt there was no need to jeopardise that Friday's Herald Express and the massive amount of advertising it contained.

Dick wandered off to see what stories the Herald Express was going to carry on top of the news about Frank Helliwell's arrest.

He sat down in the windowless office where he had found Ellen McCraken and Adrian Wall working the week before, picked up a batch of Herald Express page proofs and started reading. It came as no surprise that he found most of the stories Tim Fletcher and his team had written were less than impressive.

"Weak, lacking inspiration and boring," was the first comment he made when an hour later he returned to the boardroom from the production area. "It's a good job Harvey Fairbanks provided a decent tribute piece about Edna, because the rest of them would have been clueless."

Mary could see that underneath he was simmering. She knew he would not tolerate poor quality reporting for very long.

"I am going to catch up on some of the paper work I have neglected," he told her. "Is there anything you would like to do to pass the time?"

She realised he would benefit from a few hours on his own to catch up on what he described as 'real newspaper work'.

As far as she was concerned it was time to indulge herself with some retail therapy; she felt she had earned the time off.

"I am going to disappear for the rest of the day and go shopping in Truro," she told him. "I shall take the pool car if that is OK?"

Much to her relief, Dick declined the invitation to go with her or meet later for lunch. He was not the best companion when it came to browsing the latest fashions.

"The car is yours. I will get somebody to give me a lift back to the hotel so take your time and enjoy yourself. I think I will make a start on that over-due report for Jack Wilde," he remarked as she headed for the door.

It seemed an age ago since he had first walked through the Herald Express's front door to begin what seemed an easy enough task on behalf of the Thompson Group.

What was it his managing director had told him that sunny day in Torchester? *"A couple of weeks should be enough, but if you need a bit longer that is fine."* Since then his world had been turned upside down.

The question was where to start? He began to make a list of bullet points – the main items he felt he must include and the recommendations he would suggest to bring the Cornish papers up to scratch.

Neither Jack Wilde nor Henry Thompson liked the key points of any report to be wrapped in flowery language. He had sat in too many monthly meetings and seen other managers savaged for either using jargon, officialise or long winded phrases.

There had been one memorable, at least for him, meeting when one of the editors had talked about a cumulative impact area instead of a town centre and predictors of beaconicity instead of good ideas.

Jack Wilde had looked over the top of his glasses and with a devastating impact on those present said: "Don't you ever use such words again in my hearing, and if anything like that appears in your paper fear the worst. Never forget K.I.S.S. – keep it simple stupid."

Everyone had got the message.

Even if Dick had wanted to go shopping – and he didn't - he did not feel he could safely leave the office during normal working hours. Neither Tim Fletcher nor Lulu Popplewell disturbed him and it wasn't until he was about to return to the hotel, where he expected Mary to be enjoying a swim, that he took a phone call from DCI Lolly.

"Just to let you know Frank Helliwell has been refused bail which came as no real surprise to him. He is not being any trouble. I think he is still stunned by everything that has happened. We are looking after him and his wife has been to see him. His story better improve if he is not to spend many years in jail, but I must be going soft because I believe what he has told us. I am not sure a jury will though."

"Can I ask a favour?" said Dick.

"Fire away."

"Don't ask me to explain, but it would be really handy if you and DS Walker were to call into this office around 9.30am tomorrow."

"Ok, there are a few loose ends I need to clear up with you so we can do it then. Sleep well."

The line was cut.

Sleep is the last thing I will get tonight, thought Dick. He was wrong. After a pleasant dinner, an hour watching television and two phone calls he fell asleep soon after his head touched the pillow. He was sleeping peacefully when Mary returned from the bathroom and turned out the light.

"Sweat dreams," she whispered.

∗

The last day of the working week for most people is really the first for many local newspaper reporters and advertising reps. The paper is out, another one needs to be planned and there are calls to be made. Since Dick Chinnery's arrival nobody had turned up for work after nine o'clock unless they had had some task to carry out on the way in.

He had already asked his secretary back in Torchester not to book him and Mary on the only flight from St Mawgan to Stansted that day, but to hold onto two seats for the Saturday flight until mid afternoon when he would know for certain whether they were going to make it home for the weekend. He yearned for his own bed and familiar surroundings.

At exactly 9.25am Mary triggered the fire alarm. There were no arguments – everybody had to vacate the building. Fortunately, it was not raining. Lulu Popplewell and Tim Fletcher ushered their people out the front while Dick made it his responsibility to get the entire production team and press crew out of the back door and to their own assembly points. He told Frank Helliwell's deputy to do the roll call and to take his time as he had never done it before.

Unseen, Dick then slipped back inside the building. He knew it was perfectly safe - there was no fire. He made straight for the press crew's lockers and underneath a pair of overalls he found what he was looking for among Jonny Grayson's belongings. A quick glance revealed Edna Sparrow had written quite a bit about him.

Dick didn't have time to read all she had committed to paper – there would be enough time for that shortly.

Two fire engines duly turned up five minutes later, making quite a racket in the process. The firemen searched the building, but could not find any sign of a fire. They did all the necessary checks, but could not come to any conclusion about what had triggered the alarm. Eventually they suggested the possibility that Harvey Fairbanks might not have had the alarms tested or serviced for many years and there was a fault somewhere. Dick promised to look into it so there was no repeat incident.

At that moment DCI Lolly and DS Walker made themselves known. They had waited patiently in the car park as events had unfolded. Dick took them to the boardroom and quickly told them what he had done and why.

They scanned Edna's file on Jonny Grayson. It was enough for them to realise they just might be holding the wrong man at Broad Bottom police station.

They didn't want to risk Jonny doing a runner if he found the damning file was no longer in his locker. DCI Lolly accompanied Dick to the press room while DS Walker went to guard the back door. There was no other way out.

Jonny had not realised the papers had been taken from his locker while he was outside during the fire emergency. He was too busy sharing some gossip with another member of the press crew to notice Dick and DCI Lolly approaching him.

The senior detective didn't waste much time after the initial introductions before suggesting the pair of them had better have a longer chat somewhere more private. The other members of the press crew looked on without comment as their work colleague was marched away to the boardroom via the editorial department.

It hardly caused a stir among the journalists.

This lot wouldn't spot a story under their noses, thought Dick. It was something else for his report.

CHAPTER TWENTY TWO

"You would have done the same if you had discovered someone had written a pack of lies about you. Anyway, it is hardly a serious crime to have kept her notes in my locker," was Jonny Grayson's opening comments to DCI Lolly and DS Walker after he had been shown the file Edna Sparrow held on him.

The two detectives were happy to let him do all the talking – for the moment. They had conducted too many interviews when the other party had simply sat there, folded his arms, said 'no comment' and grinned at them.

"She was a horrible woman. I couldn't believe it when I realised what she had written about me. Ok, I have had a couple of affairs and maybe I do like to bet too much on the horses, but it was none of her business. I think she would have blackmailed all of us at some stage to get even more money."

"You can only be successfully blackmailed if you have something to hide in the first place," interjected DS Walker.

For fifteen minutes the two policemen went over old ground, probing him about the wool he and others had been pulling over the company's eyes. It was their usual warm-up act – to concentrate on making their victim realise he was no saint; to probe his weaknesses. Once they felt they had got Jonny's measure, they would move in for the kill - not just yet.

"We are going to help ourselves to a coffee, Mr Grayson. Can we get you anything?" said DCI Lolly.

Jonny didn't know whether to accept or decline. Eventually he told them he was ok.

They left the boardroom to consult and let him sweat. Dick Chinnery had provided them with a key to lock the door behind them.

"It's him alright," said DS Walker as they looked across from the reception area to where Dick and Mary were sat in the advertising department. "We have charged the wrong man in Frank Helliwell."

DCI Lolly agreed. They would have to rectify that mistake as soon as they had cracked Jonny Grayson.

They didn't bother to ask the editorial secretary to make them a coffee, but instead they took a short walk round the car park to get some fresh air. They knew the longer they left their suspect on his own the more likely it was he would be happy to talk when they returned.

When they eventually re-entered the boardroom they got straight to the point.

"We have another member of the Herald Express staff who was in the vicinity of the news room at the time of Miss Sparrow's murder and they have given us a statement," said DCI Lolly.

It wasn't a lie, but it did stretch the truth.

"They couldn't have seen me – it was too dark," blurted out Jonny without thinking.

It was enough. The time on his own had shredded his nerves. He stared at them in horror when he realised what he had just said.

DCI Lolly stood up.

"Jonny Grayson I am formally charging you with the murder of Miss Edna Sparrow. You do not have to say anything, but it may harm your defence if you do not mention when questioned something which you later rely on in court. Anything you do say may be given in evidence."

Whether it was the shock of being found out or an instinctive reaction, Jonny could not stop himself.

"I only meant to frighten her, make her realise that if she messed us around any more there would be consequences. I knew Frank was going to talk to her at eight o'clock but I didn't believe he would get anywhere - he is a pussycat, useless."

DS Walker cuffed him and told him what would happen when he was taken to the police station for further questioning.

"We have the right to take photographs of you. We will also take fingerprints and a DNA sample from a mouth swab or head hair root from you and possibly a swab from the skin surface of your hands and arms. We don't need your permission to do this. Do you understand?"

A now silent Jonny nodded.

"You have the right to free legal advice before we can question you further at a police station. We have an independent duty solicitor available or we will contact, on your behalf, a solicitor of your own choosing."

Jonny Grayson had only ever used the services of a solicitor for moving house. He was in a lost world of his own making.

DS Walker went out to make a phone call. A few minutes later a police car arrived at the Herald Express's front door. The two girls on reception could only gawk as the by now subdued member of the Herald's press crew was led out and bundled onto the back seat of the first car. DS Walker got in beside him.

Dick and Mary clearly saw what had occurred from the advertising department window. They made their way back to the boardroom where DCI Lolly awaited them.

"We will have to carry out a few minor preliminaries, but Frank Helliwell will be released as quickly as possible. Would you mind following me to the station to collect him and then take him home? I presume you won't want him to return to work today!"

Dick thought it was a good idea, but asked if he could ring Jack Wilde first. He knew just how much his boss hated hearing the news second hand.

When they reached Broad Bottom police station DCI Lolly told Dick everything Jonny Grayson had said.

"I am sure that killing Miss Sparrow was not his initial intention, but once he got the tie round her neck he couldn't stop himself. There was too much pent up anger to be released. I don't think his colleagues realised how furious he was when he discovered she was taking a bigger slice of the cake than them. When he found out what she had written about him it was too much."

Dick could only agree.

"Do you think he would have let Frank Helliwell serve a long prison term?" he asked.

"We will never know. By the way there won't be any charges pressed against you or your wife."

For once Dick was nearly speechless.

"Against us?" he gulped.

"For making that hoax call to the fire brigade. In an effort to curtail the number of such false calls we are working with the fire service and telephone companies to clamp down on offenders. In some counties they send a warning text, but here in Cornwall we are much tougher. The penalty for dialling 999 with a pretend complaint can be severe – up to a £5,000 fine or a six month jail sentence."

Dick drew a large breath, then realised the detective was having some fun at his expense. He grinned and touched the side of his nose.

DCI Lolly shook Dick's hand.

"Thank you for all your help and quick thinking. I will get most of the credit when the dust settles, but it is you and your wife who made the real breakthrough."

Thirty minutes later Frank Helliwell was even more stunned than he had been when he was first arrested. He was released from custody but barely took any notice of the police apology.

The drive to his Little Bottom home enabled Dick to bring him up to date. When they pulled up outside Mrs Helliwell came rushing out to meet them.

Dick just had time to tell Frank to take a week's holiday before she enveloped her husband in her arms and started crying again. He didn't go into the house with them; he thought the Helliwells would want to be alone.

After yet another sandwich lunch – Mary also allowed him a bag of crisps as a 'treat' – Dick called what proved to be to be his final staff meeting at the Broad Bottom Herald Express to appraise everyone of the facts, as far as he knew them, surrounding Jonny Grayson's arrest and Frank Helliwell's release.

Once again he felt it was his duty to make it clear that everyone was assumed to be innocent until proven guilty, but he soon discovered there was near unanimity at the Herald Express about Jonny Grayson's guilt. One jury, at least, had already made up its mind. He could tell there was widespread relief that Frank Helliwell was not a murderer.

Half an hour later another member of the press crew knocked on the boardroom door. He told Dick he thought the police ought to know that on that fatal Thursday night he had seen Jonny slip away for at least 15 minutes during a break to change the paper reels on the press. He made no mention of the press crew's pact to stick together at all costs.

DS Walker returned later in the day to take his statement.

Dick held one further meeting in the boardroom that Friday afternoon. He called in the three editors and Lulu Popplewell for an impromptu management meeting.

Mary felt discretion was called for so she went to another room to confirm their flight reservations which would take them home the next morning.

"I don't think my heart will take much more of the quiet life here in Cornwall," Dick said jokingly when Ellen McCraken and Adrian Wall arrived together. Tim Fletcher didn't laugh.

"As you know, I came down here to take an initial look at the business on behalf of the Thompson Group. Thank you for your help. I aim to go back to Torchester tomorrow, finish the report I have to write and let others decide what happens next."

Ellen asked whether he would be returning as their new managing director. Tim Fletcher and Adrian Wall gave her looks which indicated the very thought horrified them.

"We like Essex and Suffolk too much to uproot," he diplomatically replied. "Mary's family live near to our home in Thurnham – several of them are quite elderly."

It was a good job Mary's father could not hear him, he thought.

Tim and Adrian exchanged furtive looks. *Mary, his wife?* They had never guessed.

"I am leaving the four of you to run the business *pro tem*. I expect you to hold a weekly meeting at a time you agree between you and to send me the minutes. On pain of death you will never employ Rufus Jones in any capacity."

At last they thought they were beginning to understand his humour. The funny thing was, he wasn't joking!

"I expect you, Tim, to attend Edna's inquest which at this stage will be a formality because after some initial statements the coroner will postpone it until Jonny Grayson's trial is concluded. Oh, and before I forget, can you get the fire alarm checked, Lulu?"

*

They flew home on Saturday morning from St Mawgan hand in hand. Mary's father was at Stansted to greet them and drive them to Thurnham.

"Did you have a good holiday in Cornwall?" he asked. "Your mother and I had a couple of holidays there many years ago. I thought the coastline was beautiful but preferred Devon's interior. Some of the main towns, apart from Truro, looked very neglected."

Mary agreed with her father and because she was delighted to see him, and loved him nearly as much as she loved her husband, she did not attempt to interrupt him while he was in full flow.

"It was a bit too quiet for me and felt off the beaten track. The first time I went I thought we were just about there when we got to Exeter, but to my amazement it took us another couple of hours to reach our hotel," he added.

"It is a very sleepy part of the world where I suspect nothing really exciting happens from one year to another. How did you find the locals?"

He did not understand why his two passengers were laughing, or why they found it hard to stop.

FOOTNOTE:

- Jonny Grayson received a life sentence when he was tried for the murder of Edna Sparrow at Truro Crown Court. He died in Exeter Prison two years later after a fight with another inmate.

- Frank Helliwell and the rest of the press crew, including a new recruit, carried on taking photographs for local estate agents in their own time. However, they all received tax bills when the Inland Revenue caught up with them several months later. Frank is still production manager at the Herald Express.

- Tim Fletcher and Ellen McCraken swapped jobs after Dick Chinnery's report was accepted by the Thompson Group board of directors. She totally revamped the Herald Express. Lulu Popplewell became commercial director of all four papers.

- Edna Sparrow died intestate. Her elderly aunt died a week after her murder. To everyone's astonishment Edna's estate was valued at more than a quarter of a million pounds. After funeral expenses every penny went to the government.

- Rufus Jones is still looking for a new job on any newspaper. He drinks a lot.

- Marie-Clementine Dubois was sentenced to nine years in prison for bribery, blackmail and other charges involving state security. On her release she was deported and now lives in France where she is married to the multi-millionaire owner of a leading French football club.

- A month after Miss Dubois was arrested the private detective who had followed her was found dead in the River Thames.

- Former Deputy Chief Constable Ryan Johnston received a lesser two year sentence. At his trial the judge told him he was 'a love-sick fool.' He did not find prison a pleasant experience. He now works for an estate agent in Chelmsford.

- Arthur Nightingale is now Sir Arthur Nightingale and as far as anyone knows still works somewhere in the secret service.

- Jurgen Weber and Sergei Mudkoi were recalled by their governments. Nobody in diplomatic circles has heard anything about either of them since.

- One senior government minister and three junior ministers were sacked by PM Margaret Thatcher in a surprise government reshuffle. All four stood down at the 1987 General Election.

- Former deaconess Brea Williams and Annabel Johnston moved to Gorleston in Norfolk where they still run a whelk stall on the sea front. They send Dick Chinnery a Christmas card every year.

- Harvey Fairbanks died 18 months after he sold his newspapers to the Thompson Group.

- A month after returning home, Mary Chinnery discovered she was pregnant. She is still editor of the Thurnham and Shaldon Standard.

- Dick Chinnery has never wanted to holiday in Cornwall, but pays occasional 'flying visits' for local board meetings.

About the Author

David Scott is the former editor of several regional newspapers and was managing director of a daily newspaper in Birmingham before setting up his own media consultancy and journalism training company in 1988.

Since then more than 9,000 reporters and newspaper managers have attended one of his training courses.

He lives in Torquay with his wife, Valerie, and has three grown-up children, none of whom now live at home.

He is an avid fan of Burnley Football Club, the New England Patriots and Boston Red Sox and spends as many warm, sunny days as possible watching Somerset play cricket at Taunton.

Murder on the Herald Express is his fifth book.

Other titles include Once a Week is Enough (out of print); The Standard Bearer (the first Dick Chinnery story), The Joys and Terrors of Public Speaking and Death by a Thousand Clots.